LONGARM HIT THE GROUND HARD...

... and before he could roll aside, nine hundred pounds of dying cayuse came down on top of him.

The horse thrashed wildly for a moment, then went suddenly rigid and collapsed in dead—quite literally dead—weight directly on top of Longarm's legs.

"Son of a *bitch!*" he snarled as he tried to pull himself free.

From over toward the creek he heard a most unexpected sound. Not the report of another gunshot, but the hoofbeats of a racing horse.

Apparently the gunman had a horse hidden over there, too. Which probably meant—no, which almost certainly meant—that whoever shot at him was not one of the Druid women of Harrisonville.

The ladies might or might not be willing to act as the assassins of deputy U.S. marshals. Longarm would reserve judgment on that subject. But he was fairly sure none of them had a horse to escape on.

But who the shooter could be ... and why ... those questions would have to wait until he could work himself out from under this dead horse. Dammit!

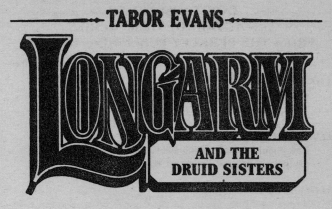

TABOR EVANS

LONGARM

AND THE DRUID SISTERS

JOVE BOOKS, NEW YORK

LONGARM AND THE DRUID SISTERS

A Jove Book / published by arrangement with
the author

PRINTING HISTORY
Jove edition / September 2002

Copyright © 2002 by Penguin Putnam Inc.

All rights reserved.
This book, or parts thereof, may not be reproduced in any form
without permission.
For information address: The Berkley Publishing Group,
a division of Penguin Putnam Inc.,
375 Hudson Street, New York, New York 10014.

Visit our website at
www.penguinputnam.com

ISBN: 0-515-13368-X

A JOVE BOOK®
Jove Books are published by The Berkley Publishing Group,
a division of Penguin Putnam Inc.,
375 Hudson Street, New York, New York 10014.
JOVE and the "J" design
are trademarks belonging to Penguin Putnam Inc.

PRINTED IN THE UNITED STATES OF AMERICA

10 9 8 7 6 5 4 3 2 1

Chapter 1

"You look mighty damned gloomy this morning, Longarm."

Deputy United States Marshal Custis Long made a sour face and deposited his brown Stetson onto a hat rack in the marshal's outer office. The fact that he walked to the rack and placed the hat onto it, rather than jauntily tossing the article across the room—he sometimes missed, but not very often—was proof that the clerk's comment was accurate.

"I don't wanta talk about it," Longarm grumbled.

Without looking up from the stack of papers on his desk, the bookish and mild looking little clerk offered, "Pull out on the late train, did she?"

Longarm shot a positively venomous glance in Henry's direction.

"The newspaper said the troupe is heading for an engagement in San Francisco, right?"

"How the hell did you know about it?" As far as Longarm was aware, nobody in Denver and certainly no one in this office knew about the dalliance he and Belle enjoyed during her show's run at the Olantha Opera House.

1

Henry looked up for the first time. And grinned. Hugely.

"Why you pip-squeak little son of a bitch!" Longarm roared. "You suckered me, didn't you? You didn't know a damn thing."

Henry, obviously not at all intimidated by Longarm's outburst, began to laugh. Loudly. But then Henry was not very easily intimidated. Despite his unimpressive appearance, he had as much brass in him as the marshal or any deputy assigned to this office, and the bulk of Henry's brass was in his balls.

He was also a good enough friend that Longarm could call him a son of a bitch without giving offense.

Longarm fumed and fussed for several minutes, then snorted and asked, "How the hell did you figure it out?"

Henry laughed again. "Custis, when was the last time a troupe of entertainers came to the city without at least one of the blondes falling head over heels for you? Don't know? I can tell you exactly. It was in July two years ago. Know how I know that? It's because that troupe came and went while you were down in New Mexico chasing a bunch of train robbers. Otherwise you'd've been sniffing up the skirts of one of that bunch, too."

Longarm shook his head in an exaggerated show of wounded feelings and false accusation. The truth, on the other hand, was that Henry was close enough to being correct that any picky little details didn't matter. Deputy Marshal Custis Long did indeed have a penchant for flamboyant ladies of the stage. And they most often reciprocated the feeling.

Long—Longarm to his friends and to a good many enemies as well—was a ruggedly masculine gent. More to the point, there was something about him, something in his appearance or demeanor or carriage, that attracted women to him like moths fluttering to a campfire's cheerful flame.

He stood several inches over six feet in height and had broad shoulders that narrowed down to lean hips and a flat belly. His features were a study in nut browns. Hair, hugely sweeping mustache, lively eyes and weathered complexion were all in brown of one shade or another.

His everyday choice of clothing normally consisted of his snuff-brown Stetson, a brown tweed coat, tan calfskin vest, light-brown checked shirt with a string tie and brown corduroy trousers. The brown was relieved by black leather cavalry boots and a black gunbelt rigged for a cross draw. The belt carried a double action Colt .44-40 while across Longarm's belly a thin gold chain was draped from one vest pocket to the other. One end of that chain was attached to a watch as one might expect, but the other was soldered not to any ordinary fob, but to a .41-caliber derringer pistol.

Far from being all appearance for the benefit of the ladies, however, Longarm was also the top deputy riding for U.S. Marshal William Vail. He could be unorthodox at times, but he was undeniably effective when it came to pursuing outlaws and bringing them to justice. Sometimes very rough justice.

"Smart-ass little son of a bitch," Longarm grumbled. But he was smiling when he said it.

Henry only laughed again.

"Is the boss in?" Longarm asked.

"Custis, you'll never see the day when you get here earlier in the morning than he does. He's been inside for the better part of an hour already."

Longarm didn't bother to ask how Henry would have that information. He already knew. Henry probably was here at his desk before Billy Vail walked in this morning. "Glad I don't have that kinda dedication," he commented. "But then I had t' stay up late last night t' see a train off." He winked at Henry and enjoyed the mildly envious look that was Henry's response.

Henry cleared his throat and said, "He told me to send you in if you ever decided to show up and do some work."

Longarm took a moment to drag the watch out of his pocket and consult it. He was only twenty minutes late. And twenty minutes, hell, that was practically the same as being early. For him. "I suppose," he said, "since I don't have anything better t' do. . . ."

He went to the door that separated Billy Vail's private office from the much larger area where the deputies liked to avoid work and tapped lightly to announce himself.

The boss was at his desk. Of course, it seemed that Billy was always at his desk these days. Longarm's personal and private opinion was that a U.S. Marshal's job was a real pisser. All paperwork and politics with no time to get out and chase felons. And hell, it was the chasing that was the fun in the job. For sure it wasn't the money.

No, marshals might earn a whole helluva lot more than deputies did, but the fact was that Custis Long wouldn't have traded jobs with Billy for all the money in the Denver Mint.

"So tell me," Longarm challenged. "What's so damned important that I have t' crawl outa bed before noon to find out about it?"

Billy took a look in the direction of the clock on the wall behind Longarm's head. "Just barely before noon, I see," the balding marshal said in a slow drawl that betrayed his Texas roots. Before coming to Colorado to serve as marshal here in Denver, Billy had been a Texas Ranger. The man had more than enough sand in his craw to earn the respect of the deputies under his command.

"It ain't eight o'clock yet," Longarm protested.

"Oh, so you *do* know what time it is," Billy said, rather smugly.

Trapped. For a lousy twenty minutes, Longarm was trapped. Billy liked to have his deputies in the office by

4

seven-thirty. It was a wish seldom realized in Longarm's case.

Longarm ignored the comment. All Billy said was, "Sit down. I have an assignment for you."

That, Longarm thought, was more like it. Henry had taken the edge off his bad mood already. And now Billy was going to give him some work to do. That would go a long way toward getting him over the disappointment of seeing that train full of lovelies pull away from the station in the wee hours this morning.

Longarm dragged a pencil-thin cheroot out of his pocket and began the rather laborious process of trimming and lighting it, absorbing the boss's introductory comments while he did so.

Longarm might well be a smart-ass a good bit of the time while he was here in the Denver federal building. But when it came to the performance of his duties, all that was set aside and he turned serious. Deadly serious as often as not.

Chapter 2

"Our worthy brothers over at the Post Office have requested our help with a small problem that they think they may have." Billy paused. "Or not."

"Oh, that sounds nice and explicit," Longarm commented dryly, a plume of smoke trickling out of the corner of his mouth and curling toward the ceiling.

Billy smiled. "Wait. It gets better."

"I think I'm thrilled already, Boss."

"What they tell me is that a town has been incorporated in Crawford County, Wyoming. The name of the town"— Billy had to find a piece of paper among several on his desk and refer to it before he went on—"the name of this new community is Harrisonville."

"Never heard of it," Longarm admitted.

"No one had until late last fall. That is when the town was incorporated and listed with the territorial government. The filing was made"—he found another sheet and glanced at it—"last November, if that makes any difference."

"All right." Longarm couldn't see any reason to care. But then, you never knew which scrap of seemingly insignificant information might prove to be important. His theory was that the more facts you had, the more likely you were to possess that one critical one when the need arose.

"Requests were made for the appointment of a postmaster and a contract mail carrier. Those requests were filed simultaneously with the incorporation. The postmaster, a gentleman named B. F. Lily, was appointed three days later. Three weeks after that, on December second, a contract was awarded to the Hysop Express Company to transport mail in and out."

"Three weeks seems mighty sudden, don't it?"

"I thought the same thing. The deputy assistant postmaster general explained—at least insofar as he understood the situation—there is no other freight or express company servicing Harrisonville. And the company offered to accept a lower than standard fee for services."

Longarm raised an eyebrow.

"Uh huh. Seemed odd to me, too. In exchange for the reduced payment they negotiated a monthly retainer, a minimum payment whether mail is actually carried or not."

The eyebrow flicked upward again.

"Apparently the good people with the Hysop Express Company knew something that the postmaster general did not."

"How's that?" Longarm asked.

"Because in the months since the postmaster was appointed and the mail contract issued, not one piece of mail has moved into or out of Harrisonville, Wyoming, and not one single cent has been remitted to the postmaster general's office to represent stamps sold."

"More than a trifle odd, I'll agree."

"Yes. The postmaster general's office certainly thinks so."

"Fine. But why would they bother us with it? Seems a simple enough deal t' me. They have auditors, don't they?

Ask one o' them to go look at the books at the post office there. Have 'em question this Hysop outfit and the Harrisonville postmaster, too. I can't see any reason why we should be involved."

"Longarm, I know you are not as stupid as you would sometimes like me to believe. I am sure it has already occurred to you that post offices are not created and mail contracts let in a matter of days for just anyone. Someone—and I have no idea who—but someone involved in this situation in Wyoming has strong political clout."

Billy frowned. "This is made all the more difficult because Wyoming is a territory and not a sovereign state. So, the political machines there will necessarily have their roots in the District of Columbia. Someone in the halls of Congress—perhaps even higher up than that—must surely be the sponsor who greased the skids and made all this speed and efficiency possible.

"And, as you know, Longarm, our brethren in the post office are, shall we say, sensitive to the blowing of political winds."

"And we aren't?" Longarm asked. He knew better, of course. *All* federal agencies are influenced by politics to one degree or another.

"There are advantages to being a maverick, Longarm. There are also disadvantages. Somehow, I seem to have acquired the reputation of being something of a maverick."

Longarm grinned. Fact was, Billy Vail just didn't give a shit. Right was right, and wrong was wrong, and the hell with anybody who wanted to mix the two together. The amazement was not that U.S. Marshal William Vail was known to be a maverick, but that he managed to remain in office in spite of that. But then the deputy attorney general who oversaw such matters was an uncommonly sensible fellow who valued performance above

8

politics. It amazed Longarm that he continued in office, too.

"Anyway, rightly or wrongly, Longarm, I agreed to investigate the situation in Harrisonville."

"You say you are gonna investigate?"

"Through the good offices of my deputy, of course," Billy said with a smugly self-satisfied smile. "Naturally, if anything goes wrong, you will take the blame for your errors. But . . ."

"But if it all works just fine, you get the credit," Longarm finished for him.

Both men laughed.

"Just as a small aside, Boss, d'you have any idea where this Harrisonville place is?"

"Certainly. I already told you. In Crawford County."

Longarm rolled his eyes skyward. Crawford County, Wyoming, was bigger than half a dozen states back east of the Mississippi. "I'll find it," he said.

"I have every confidence that you will. Consider that task the first part of your investigation."

"Yeah, well, I needed something nice an' easy t' occupy myself with for the next little while." He stood.

"Between lady friends, are you?" Billy ventured.

"You and that nosy damn clerk of yours," Longarm complained. "Two peas in a pod, ain't you?"

"Just don't waste too much time up there. Doing a favor for the deputy assistant postmaster general is one thing, Longarm, but letting it get in the way of real work would be carrying it too far. Go take a look, write out a report, and maybe by the time you get back I will have something important for you."

"Whatever you say, Boss." He faked a yawn and winked. "An' thank you very much for this vacation opportunity." With that, he headed out to retrieve his hat and go make sure his bag was packed, ready for travel.

Chapter 3

Cheyenne. If you wanted to go anywhere in Wyoming Territory, you pretty much had to go through Cheyenne to get there. Longarm had taken a night train north—with Belle on the road there was no reason for him to remain in Denver overnight—and so reached Cheyenne fairly early in the morning. He collected his bag and saddle and hiked into town in search of an agent for the Hysop Express Company.

There wasn't one.

"Look, mister, I'm telling you, I never heard of them. Know why I'm telling you that? Because, damn it, I never heard of them. Honest. I got no reason to lie to you about it."

"Sorry," Longarm said. "I didn't mean to question you. I'm just surprised, that's all."

The agent for the Overland Express grunted an acknowledgment of the apology, but did not look much happier for it.

"This town I'm looking for, it's in Crawford County, up the other side of . . ."

"I know where Crawford County is," the clerk said, sounding more than a little bit testy.

"Right." Longarm stopped short of saying sorry again. It is one thing to apologize, another to go overboard about it.

"I can get you to Buffalo. That's in Johnson County."

Longarm refrained from pointing out that he already knew where Buffalo was. He'd given this man enough grief already and didn't want to seem snotty about the confusion.

"From there or maybe from Cade's Station between Buffalo and Sheridan they'll be able to get you over to Crawford County. What did you say the name of that town is, mister?"

Longarm reminded him, but the man only shook his head. "Nope. Haven't heard of a Harrisonville any more than I have of a Hysop Express. But if this place is in Crawford County, somebody in Buffalo ought to know, and Charlie Boyd at Cade's Station would know for certain sure. The only road into Crawford from the east runs through Cade's, so Charlie will know, if anybody in this territory does."

"All right, good."

"I can ticket you through to Cade's Station if you want."

"Overland goes there?"

The agent shook his head. "No, but there's a couple different stagecoach lines that do. We broker for all of them, so I can arrange your ticket right here. Give me a minute to check the schedules, and I'll see if I can't get you on your way as quick as this afternoon."

"That would be fine, thanks."

The agent spent a good ten minutes researching the carriers and schedules, then returned with a look of satisfaction. "The Julesburg and Virginia City Coach Lines can take you. Your coach will pull out at two-thirty this afternoon. They board passengers at the dead cottonwood three blocks west of here, the same tree where they hung

11

Chucky Martin and Lou Jasper last fall. You know the spot?"

"I know it," Longarm assured him.

The agent smiled and rooted through a drawer beneath the counter searching for the particular ticket book he needed. "That will be . . . let me see here . . . eleven dollars and seventeen cents. You'll change coaches in Casper, and you can lay over there or in Buffalo if you like, no extra charge."

Longarm cleared his throat and laid his wallet onto the counter, opened to show his badge. "Federal employee," he said. "With pass privileges."

The Overland agent looked like he wasn't sure if he should shriek or maybe cry. All that, and he wasn't going to make a cent off of it.

Longarm touched the brim of his Stetson and nodded. "Thank you, mister. You been mighty kind."

He wasn't entirely sure, but he thought he could make out some of the words the agent was mumbling as Longarm made his way back out onto the street.

Probably it was just as well that he wasn't quite positive about most of them or he might've felt compelled to take offense.

By the time Longarm reached Casper, he'd been traveling for more than forty-eight hours and hadn't slept in considerably longer—although he'd caught a few restless catnaps between jolts and lurches as first the train and then a stagecoach carried him north.

After all, that last night he'd had in Denver before he was given this job was the last night he could expect to be with Belle for a long time. And the truth was that he hadn't devoted a whole helluva lot of that night to sleeping, either.

The layover that ticket agent back in Cheyenne had mentioned was sounding better and better to him. And it wasn't like this was the sort of assignment that had any urgency attached. Neither Harrisonville nor its post office were going anywhere. Or, if for some reason they did, well, that would resolve the issue and Longarm could go home again.

The Julesburg and Virginia City coach rumbled to a halt at the stage station on the outskirts of Casper, and the passengers stepped wearily down. Most of them headed around toward the back of the building where the crappers would be found. Coffee and something to eat could wait. Longarm was the only one who climbed onto the roof and fetched down his luggage.

"Thought you was going on from here, Marshal," the shotgun messenger said.

"I am," Longarm told the man, "but I think I'll lay over here until tomorrow." He smiled. "No offense, but a man can't enjoy but just so much of this punishment."

"You do whatever you're a mind to, Marshal, but there's no coach scheduled tomorrow. Next northbound isn't till the day after. We don't run 'em but every other day, y'see."

Longarm shrugged. "I can live with that."

"Want some advice then?"

"Sure." Only a fool thinks he knows more than everybody around him, and bad advice needn't be taken, just politely listened to.

"The hotel you can see over there is the one most everybody heads for when they get off the coach. 'Cause it's close and easy to see, I suppose."

"Yes?"

"You don't wanta stay there. The man that runs it doesn't change his sheets but every couple weeks or so and doesn't seem to change his mattress stuffing hardly ever. If you sleep there, you get an awful lot of little bitty livestock for company overnight."

13

"Do you have any suggestions about where I should go?" Longarm asked.

"I always stay at the Widow Jeffries' boardinghouse when I'm here, but there's plenty other places in town where a man can hire himself a bed. There's another hotel down the other end of the street, and a couple of the bigger saloons have rooms, too. With or without companionship, if you know what I mean."

"And if I go to this widow's place, should I tell her who sent me?"

The fellow laughed and shook his head. "You mean am I telling you this so's she'll give me a tip or something. The answer is no, there's no such deal as that. Hell, if you gave her my name, she wouldn't know who you was talking about. I just figured you seem a nice enough fella that I'd steer you right. Besides, truth is that I've always wanted to be a lawman myself. A U.S. deputy marshal . . . you fellas are kind of like my idols. You're the best."

"Ever carry a badge?"

"No, sir. This job here is as close as I've ever come."

"Tell you what then. You've steered me right about the layover, so let me return the favor. I hear the railroad is going to be looking to hire some more railroad detectives soon. They put the word around Denver looking for recommendations or if, like, any of our boys want to get into something not quite so dangerous. You might try there. Anybody with experience as a stagecoach shotgun messenger and a railroad detective, too, won't have any trouble finding work as a deputy someplace if he decides he wants to stick with it."

The man grinned. "Thank you, Marshal. Thanks a lot."

"If you decide to apply when you get back to Cheyenne, tell them Custis Long recommended you. Might do you some good." He smiled. "Or not."

"Long? You're Long*arm*? And you were on my stage

14

this whole time? Oh, my. Oh, my goodness gracious. Thank you, Marshal. Thank you."

Longarm escaped from the fellow's effusive gratitude by picking up his bag and saddle and heading into town in search of a place where he might get a good long sleep. After all, he'd want to be at his best when he took on so difficult a task as looking to see if there was really a post office in this Harrisonville place. Which he supposed was what this job pretty much amounted to. If the assistant deputy ass-wiper back in Denver wanted anything more than that, he could come do it himself.

Chapter 4

Longarm felt like somebody'd filled his head with wet sand. He was groggy and disoriented and apt to punch the first poor son of a bitch who smiled at him. He'd stretched out on the boardinghouse bed—clean and free of vermin, just like that shotgun messenger said it would be—with the intention of resting there for just a minute. Half a minute. Then he would get up and go find something to eat. Now it was dark outside, and he must have been asleep for hours.

Feeling so rotten after his nap was the result of sleeping too deeply for too short a time. Tomorrow he would feel just fine. Tonight was another story.

He had two choices. He could get up now and keep himself active until his head cleared, and he became tired again. Or he could try to go back to sleep and this time plan on staying there until morning. Going back to sleep again now seemed damn-all unlikely as whatever'd wakened him did a fine job of it. Better, he decided, to get up and go downstairs. He wasn't sure what time it was, but maybe the widow lady was still serving supper.

He rose and rinsed at least some of the vile taste from his mouth with a sip of water from the pitcher beside the

16

washbasin, then spit it out rather than swallow anything that nasty. There was no telling what kind of green scum might've sluiced off his tongue. At least that's what it felt and tasted like.

Longarm was careful to avoid looking at himself in the cracked mirror hanging over the wash stand. He used the palms of both hands to smooth his hair down, then retrieved his Stetson and gunbelt before venturing out into the dimly-lighted hallway and down an even more dimly-illuminated staircase.

Still in time for supper? Not hardly. There was neither sight nor sound of Mrs. Jeffries nor any of the other boarders. A single lamp burned in the vestibule, its wick turned barely high enough to allow a flame. The rest of the place was dark and silent.

Longarm made very certain the door was unlocked before he ventured outside into the cool and gently moving night air.

This part of town was dark and silent, working folk getting their sleep before another day's work come the sunrise. Some blocks away, however, he could see a spill of yellow lamplight on the rutted dirt street, and he thought he could hear distant sounds of laughter and piano . . . he couldn't call it music . . . piano playing.

He stepped down off the boardinghouse porch and headed toward the sounds of late-night merriment.

In any part of the United States, Canada, Mexico and, as far as he knew, anywhere else in the world, one saloon is pretty much like another. Oh, the exact arrangement of things will vary from one to another. But the smells are always of beer, smoke and sawdust, the sound is always of brittle laughter and loud music, the patrons always men whose faces reflect loneliness rather than contentment.

That could be considered a harsh assessment, but Longarm did not exempt himself from it. He was a man very much alone here, caring about no one in this town nor cared about by anyone here.

It was a life he was accustomed to. He did not mind it, even enjoyed it. Most of the time. But tonight his head ached and his belly growled, and he was conscious of the loneliness that was his lot as he traveled always alone, always someone's adversary.

"Whiskey. Rye if you've got it. Maryland rye if there's a choice."

"Got some comes outa Philadelphia," the barman offered.

"Close enough, friend. I'll have a glass." He laid a quarter on the bar. The gent in the apron poured a glass full and took the quarter without returning any change. Fair enough. If he'd worried about the cost, he could have asked for the bar whiskey made from raw alcohol, creek water and whatever other additives came to hand.

The whiskey cut the fur off his tongue, sweetened the taste in his mouth and banked the fires of hunger that burned in his belly. "Ah, that's good." He had another swallow that tasted even better than the first and laid a second quarter down. "Anyplace a man could get something to eat at this hour?" he asked.

"My woman might still have some mutton stew she could heat for you," the bartender said. He obviously noticed Longarm's grimace at the thought of mutton and quickly added, "Or, if you don't mind pepper-gut fixings, you could have chili *verde*, instead. She makes a good chili *verde* but not everybody likes Meskin food."

"Mutton in the chili?"

"Pork."

"I'll have the chili verde," Longarm told him, "and thank you."

"Pick a spot to sit. She'll bring it out right away." He grunted and permitted himself a small smile. "She keeps that pot on the stove alla time."

18

Longarm chose a table in a far corner where he would have walls behind him on both sides and tilted his chair back so he could survey the room and sip at the good rye whiskey. He was feeling considerably better already.

And even better still when a young, slender and exceptionally pretty Mexican woman appeared carrying a tray. Lucky man that bartender, Longarm thought, but of course refrained from saying.

The girl—she was little older than that—had gleaming black hair that hung loose below her waist and swayed when she walked. Longarm never had been able to figure out why American women insisted on pinning their hair into clumps and knots and tangles. Pretty hair was a woman's finest feature, and, in his opinion, oughtn't to be hidden or messed with.

"Senor." Her smile was dazzling, and when she bent forward to deliver his supper, her hair swung down like a cascade of black silk.

"Thank you." He could feel himself growing hard, but fortunately below the tabletop where she would not see and become embarrassed.

The girl turned, her skirts swirling, and disappeared again somewhere in the back of the place. Longarm turned his attention to the food instead.

The green chili was thick with mild peppers and chunks of tender pork and smelled so good it must have been created in heaven's kitchens, not some pisshole saloon in Casper, Wyoming Territory. It was served with a plate of steaming hot tortillas, and on another plate a pair of puffy sopaipillas dripping with honey. He found himself being pleased now that he'd slept through supper at the boardinghouse, for there was no way that could have been near as fine as this meal.

Longarm dropped his hat onto the vacant chair on his right and dug into the chow with pleasure.

Chapter 5

"Something you want, miss?" He'd finished his meal and pushed the plates away. At least she'd waited that long to make her pitch.

The woman laughed and said, "No, honey, it's you that's wanting something."

"I see. Now how d'you figure that?" He caught the bartender's eye and held a finger up, looked at the woman who'd helped herself to a seat beside him and changed his mind. He held up the second finger to call for a drink for her, too. What the hell. She was polite enough about it.

She laughed again, the sound of it light and seemingly genuine, although she would have had a great deal of practice at the arts of pretense, and said, "I saw that bulge in your britches when Maria Juana brought your food, sweetie. You're so horny, I'm surprised you aren't honking. The thing is, honey, Maria Juana doesn't go with the customers. But I do."

She made a parody of fluttering her eyelashes and sticking her chest out so that the tops of her tits showed at the neck of her blouse. At least she had a sense of humor about herself. Longarm liked that. Most women, whores included, take themselves almighty serious.

And really, she wasn't that bad a looking woman, either. Likely on the downhill side of thirty, but still with reasonably smooth, taut skin underneath the obligatory powder and rouge. Blonde hair done up in tight twists— there was that thing again, an American woman failing to recognize her greatest asset—and a scandalously short skirt. She wore a cameo on a black ribbon tied tight around her throat. The cameo was cheap, polished onyx instead of ivory. She smelled of perfume but only faintly, and she looked like she bathed nice and regular. If Longarm'd been interested in paying for pussy tonight, he would have been satisfied enough to choose her.

He opened his mouth to tell her exactly that, but was interrupted by a rather large gent in a suitcoat and derby hat who stepped up to the table behind the woman. Longarm looked up at the fellow. "Something you want, friend?"

The man did not answer. Ignoring Longarm, he balled his meaty right hand and sent a sweeping, roundhouse blow onto the side of the whore's neck.

The woman turned suddenly pale and toppled off her chair to the floor.

"Bitch!" the man—he was for damn sure no gent, Longarm concluded now—spat loudly. He drew his right foot back preparatory to a kick that he almost certainly intended to deliver somewhere on the woman's unprotected back as she lay only partially conscious in the sawdust.

He did not have time to complete that intention, however, for he found himself off balance, Longarm's right hand squeezing tight on his throat and a pair of suddenly cold eyes glaring into his from nose-to-nose distance.

"The lady," Longarm said, as calmly as if they were

having a chat about the price of beef in Kansas City, "was speaking with me."

"Let me go, mister, or I'll do the same to you."

"No," Longarm said in a deceptively mild tone of voice, "because you're in front o' me, not creeping up behind. And I ain't no woman you can overpower." By way of illustration, Longarm squeezed a little harder and with that same grip lifted the man onto his tiptoes. Longarm guided him tottering backward until the back of his head rapped sharply against the wall. The fellow's derby was knocked off and landed upside down in the sawdust. The man began to choke and gasp for breath. His right hand began to move as well.

"Don't be naughty now," Longarm admonished, reaching down with his own left to take a good grip on the web of the man's right hand. He squeezed. Hard. The man turned pale, and a nickel-plated rimfire revolver tumbled onto the floor with a small thump.

"I di . . . I . . . shi . . . I . . ." The man wheezed and sputtered, but he couldn't get any words out past Longarm's hold on his throat.

Longarm let the fellow slide down the wall far enough that his heels touched the floor again, then very slightly eased his grip on the throat. "You wanted to tell me something?"

"I . . . yeah . . . no . . . no offense. Y'know? No offense."

"Too late," Longarm said, quietly.

"No, I . . . really . . . I wasn't meaning to give offense."

Longarm glanced toward the whore, who by now had recovered sufficiently to pull herself back onto the chair. She reached out for what few drops remained of Longarm's second drink—the bartender hadn't delivered fresh ones yet and was probably intending to stay well out of whatever ruckus was happening over here—and gulped the whiskey down. Her face was flushed, and she was going to have one jimdandy of a bruise on her neck by morning.

"It's just a guess," Longarm said, "but I'd bet the lady found it offensive. An', like I said . . . she was talking to me at the time. That means that I do, indeed, take offense."

"I didn't mean. . . . You don't know this woman, mister. She shouldn't ought to be here."

"You own the place, do you?"

"No, no I . . . I provide certain . . . services. You know what I mean?"

"You're a whoremonger," Longarm suggested.

"That isn't . . . isn't what I'd call it. I'm a businessman. That's all. A businessman, don't you see?"

"Oh, I think I'm beginning to see. You run the whores in town. You want to control all the whores in town. An' this girl here isn't paying your share from what she makes. Am I getting close?"

"I . . . sure. Close enough, mister. If you want to put it that way."

"Are you aware that involuntary servitude is not legal in this country?" Longarm asked.

"This isn't. . . . She's a whore, for God's sake . . . mister, don't squeeze like that, okay? It hurts."

"Believe me," Longarm said. "I can make you hurt a whole lot worse than this." He smiled when he said it, but there was no hint of mirth in the expression. He raised the man back onto tiptoes, and the fellow began sputtering and choking again. "Or I could just put you away in jail for a spell. What would happen to the rest of your girls then? D'you think they would stick with you if you were in jail and couldn't get at them to keep them pounded into line?" He paused for only a moment, then squeezed again and asked, "Would they?"

"Mister, I. . . ." He couldn't get the words out, so Longarm let him down onto firm footing again. "Thank you. I . . .

I haven't done anything wrong, mister. Nothing I could be charged with. Go ahead and report me if you want. They won't arrest me."

"Paying off the locals, are you? Don't let that make you feel smug, buster. I can charge you with assault on a federal employee. And I could make it stick. Put you away for one to three." He gave the man that cold smile again. "Trust me. You'll be happier if you don't fuck with me."

The whoremonger sent a truly venomous glance toward the woman seated at Longarm's table, but he offered no opposition to the grown man who so easily overpowered him. "I won't. . . . Just let me go, all right? I'll walk out of here. You won't see me again."

"That sounds just fine," Longarm told him. "You don't fuck with me and you don't bother the lady. Not again. D'you understand me? Leave her alone. You do that, and everything will be just fine."

"Yes . . . yes, I . . . I'll do that. No more trouble. That's a promise."

Longarm smiled and stepped back, releasing his hold on the man's throat. The fellow's knees buckled, and he leaned against the wall for a few moments taking deep breaths and pushing them out again so he could gulp for more. After a bit, he straightened and began to reach down for the little Ivor Johnson revolver that lay half buried in the sawdust on the floor.

"Leave that," Longarm said.

The man hesitated, then apparently considered the big Colt that rested secure but ready at Longarm's waist. "Yes, sir." He stood upright, gave one more exceptionally ugly look at the woman, then turned and scurried out of the saloon.

The other customers, who had been staring silently throughout the potentially explosive encounter, went back to their own drinks, and the bartender quickly brought over the two Longarm had ordered considerably earlier.

Longarm picked up the little revolver and looked it over. It was a .32 rimfire with five chambers in the cylinder, all of them loaded although with ammunition old enough that the lead bullets had oxidized to a heavy gray patina. He handed the little gun to the woman and said, "Stick this away somewhere that you can get to nice and quick if need be."

"Thank you, mister. You saved me from a beating."

"No, I'm afraid all I really did was to make it worse when it does happen. A son of a bitch like that will blame you for me shaming him in public like I done. I owe you an apology."

"No, really, I appreciate what you did. Most men would think it was none of their business and anyway not care if some whore got thumped. You . . . you stood up for me, mister. That's a kindness that I won't forget." She paused. "I'd like to give you a present. Could I do that?"

"You don't owe me nothing."

"It isn't a matter of owing. It's a matter of wanting to. Would you let me give you something by way of a thank-you?"

She sounded genuinely grateful. And it would have been very rude of him to refuse something that she so obviously did want to give. Longarm nodded. "It's nice of you to offer, and I'd be proud to accept a gift from you, miss."

She smiled and stood. "Come with me then. Please."

Longarm grabbed for his Stetson and followed her through the silently watching saloon and out into the night.

Chapter 6

"My name is Sarah Osten, mister. My real name, that is. Everybody here knows me as French Jenny."

"Pleased t' meet you, Sarah. My name is Custis, but my friends call me Longarm." He smiled. "I'd be proud if you'd call me Longarm." He removed his hat and hung it on a knob on the ladderback rocker that sat in a corner of her bedroom.

Sarah lived and worked in a one-room shanty behind a row of large and respectable looking homes. The place was small, but he noticed that it was also clean and tidy. Engravings cut out of newspapers and magazines from back East decorated the walls, and a jumble of skillfully embroidered pillows lay on the bed. "Nice," he said, pointing to the pillows. "Did you do them?"

The woman blushed a little and bobbed her head. "In my free time. You know how it is."

"Sure." Truth was that he didn't know all that much about what a small town whore's life would be like, but there seemed no point in going into that.

"Would you like something to drink, Longarm? Or . . . anything?"

"Reckon I'll pass on the drink," he told her. "But I'd

be pleased t' have that 'anything' you mentioned." He drew her close and held her tight against him for a moment, but ignored a fleeting impulse to kiss her. No man in his right mind would kiss any whore, especially one known as Frenchy or any version of the moniker. It would be too much like taking a drink out of a cuspidor.

Sarah seemed inordinately pleased to be hugged. After a moment, she sighed and pulled slightly away from him, then began slowly unbuttoning his vest and shirt and trousers.

She had a good body for a woman her age. Her tits had begun to lose that high, proud, perky jut of youth, but they didn't actually sag yet. She was a trifle thick in the thighs, but her belly was flat enough and her waist and ankles pleasantly small. The really surprising thing was that she was a genuine blonde, her pubic hair every bit as pale as the hair on her head.

"Would you do me a favor?" he asked.

"Anything you want, Longarm. I'll suck you, of course. You already know that. If you want it up my ass . . . ," she hesitated for only a moment, ". . . sure. That, too."

Longarm laughed. "What I have in mind, Sarah, is that I'd appreciate it if you'd take your hair down and brush it out. I do like to see a woman wear her hair natural."

"Lordy, Longarm, if every man was all that easy to please, I'd be one very happy girl."

"Now mind, I didn't say that was the *only* thing I'm wanting of you tonight," Longarm added.

"Well, thank goodness for that." She'd gotten him down to his drawers at that point and peered with professional approval at what she found waiting there. Longarm had a boner that was so ready it was bouncing with every heartbeat. "Dear me. It's beautiful. And so big." She sounded quite happy about those facts.

Sarah leaned down and licked the head of his cock, then

laughed with delight at the way her moist touch made it jump. She stood upright and took him by the hand, tugging him in the direction of the large bed that dominated the room.

Longarm did not require a whole lot of urging.

She guided him onto his back, laying him in the center of the bed, then took the fancy pillows and tucked them behind his head so he could comfortably watch while she crossed the room to a low dressing table where boxes and tiny bottles and a hand mirror lay.

Quickly, she unpinned her hair and let it fall in a cascade of gold that reached below her waist.

"It's a criminal act to confine hair that pretty," Longarm said. "And if it ain't, then it oughta be."

Sarah produced a comb and brush from a drawer and patiently began stroking that long spill of gleaming yellow. Her breasts rose and fell with the movements of her hand and arm. The planes of her back bunched and shifted beneath the skin with each movement, also. She was in no hurry about this task, obviously aware of the effect she was having on Longarm, for he could see her peeking at him in the mirror from time to time. Despite the time that passed, Longarm's erection remained hard enough to drive nails.

"Better?" she asked when she finally set the comb and brush down onto the dressing table and stood, turning to face him.

"Perfect," he assured her, which brought a smile to her face.

Sarah joined him on the bed then, kneeling at his side and leaning over him. For a moment, Longarm feared she was going to kiss him. But she knew better. Of course, she did.

Instead she bent to him and carefully licked inside one ear and then the other. He could smell her breath and it was sweet, in spite of her nickname. She obviously took pains with herself. He liked that.

The sensation of her tongue in his ears was splendid. Better, she did not stop there. Sarah rolled him onto his side and licked the back of his neck. Then onto his belly so her tongue, mobile and warm and wet, could begin slowly working down his spine. Onto the cheeks of his ass. Probing into the crack and pausing to flutter and explore his asshole as well.

Longarm wasn't sure he could keep from spurting his seed onto the bedcover when she did that, but Sarah must have been able to gauge his reactions for she stopped just short of his climax and sent her tongue roving onward down his legs.

She stopped again at his feet, taking each toe in turn into her mouth and sucking it as if it were a miniature cock, then licking the valleys between his toes as well before turning him onto his back and resuming her tongue's delightful journey.

When she reached his upper thighs, she jumped over the massive tent pole that stood upright from the middle of his body and went back to his ears. The tip of her tongue probed briefly into each of his nostrils, amazing him anew that her breath remained fresh. Across his jaw then and onto his neck. Down again to his chest, lingering long at each nipple where she licked and suckled, the feeling of that again driving him to the brink of coming. She licked his belly and the interior of his navel.

Finally—at long and delicious last—she began licking and sucking his balls. The shaft of his cock. The head.

And then, mercifully, Sarah's lips parted and she took him into the wet, hot depths of her mouth.

Longarm cried aloud as the sensations became too much to contain and within seconds he felt the hot, sweet burst of shooting jism.

Sarah laughed and gurgled quite happily as she drank down the fluids that burst from him.

"Damn!" Longarm complained. "I didn't want t' come that quick."

"Don't worry, sweetie. We have plenty of time, and I can promise you we can do this again and again. As much as you can stand, all right?" She chuckled. "By the time you leave me, Longarm, I want you so loose and weak you'll walk like a drunk sailor ashore for the first time in months. With your permission, of course." She laughed again.

It seemed a helluva deal. Longarm reached down and gently stroked the hair that lay spread in a golden fan across his thighs and lower belly.

At this point he wouldn't take any bets that Sarah couldn't do exactly what she said she would. And if weak knees were the price he'd have to pay for all this pleasure, well, so be it.

He fondly touched her cheek. And guided her mouth back to his temporarily flaccid but already stirring cock.

Chapter 7

Longarm's timing was perfect. He made it back to the boardinghouse just as breakfast was being put onto the table. The Widow Jeffries gave him a baleful look and slammed a bowl of hominy down so hard it was a wonder it didn't break.

"Been out carousing all night, have you?" she accused.

The Widow Jeffries was, well, not what most men would call attractive. Maybe she was rich, though. That could account for the fact that some poor son of a bitch married her. But Longarm suspected the fellow was mighty happy to die when his time came, just so he wouldn't have to wake up to Mrs. Jeffries' face every morning. Longarm smiled at her just the same, as if she was a normal female person, and, with a wink, motioned for her to join him in the foyer while the other residents dug fast and heavy into the food.

The woman came along, sniffing loudly and tipping her head back so she could stare down her nose at him. He was grateful she was able to see well enough to keep her footing. If she'd tripped and fallen, he might've had to put his arms around her in order to prevent injury. And

31

doing that would surely have hurt his feelings, if not his reputation.

Once he got her away from the others, he glanced around as if making sure no one was close enough to overhear, then whispered, "You do remember, don't you, that I'm a deputy U.S. marshal?"

She sniffed again. "Certainly. There is nothing wrong with my memory, young man, and I . . ." She stopped and, after a moment of silence, clasped her hand over her mouth. "Do you mean to tell me you've been working on a case? Are you investigating someone here?"

Longarm laid a cautionary finger over his lips. "I didn't say any such a thing, now did I, ma'am? Not that anyone is likely t' ask. But . . . you know . . . just in case."

The widow's eyes became wide. "Oh my. No. No, indeed. I never heard you utter a peep about . . . could you tell me who?" She sounded mighty eager.

Longarm glanced furtively around again, then very solemnly shook his head. "No, ma'am. And mind now. I've not said one word t' you about there even bein' any sort o' investigation going on here."

"Yes. Oh my, yes. Of course."

"Will it be all right if I go in an' have a bite t' eat now, ma'am? It's been a long night, and I'm hungry." Which was entirely true. As were his previous comments about *not* commenting on the existence of an investigation here in Casper. He simply refrained from mentioning *why* it had been such a long and strenuous night.

"Yes. Yes, of course. Please. And Marshal. . . ."

"Yes, ma'am?"

"If the breakfast is not to your liking, you can wait until my other gentlemen have finished and gone off to work. I'll cook you whatever you like."

"Thank you, ma'am. You're very kind."

The old biddy beamed as if she'd just been given a medal.

Longarm returned to the dining room and thoroughly enjoyed a huge breakfast, then went upstairs to get a little sleep. He had the entire day to kill since the next stage to Buffalo wouldn't come through until tomorrow afternoon, and he wanted to be fresh for this evening, again.

Longarm woke about the time the sun was sinking out of sight, yawned and pulled his clothes on. The town barber was likely closed already so he bathed out of the water pitcher and basin in his room and shaved with the water that remained. A cold water shave may not be quite as comfortable as hot towels and lather, but it does the job just as well.

He went downstairs for supper—breakfast so far as his belly was concerned—then winked at Mrs. Jeffries and whispered, "Could be late again t'night."

"That is perfectly all right, Deputy. And if you need anything when you get back, just let me know. Food. Medicines. Anything."

"You're mighty kind, ma'am. Thank you." He settled the brown Stetson onto his head and let himself out into the warm, evening air.

Sarah had said she would be available any time he came by. It was damned nice of her, but costly for her to give up a night's work just so she could be nice to him. Longarm decided he would leave a little gift with her come morning. Not a whore's fee. But a measure of appreciation. He kind of liked the woman and didn't want to see her suffer on his account.

He thought about stopping for a drink first, but Sarah's place was closer than the saloon where he'd first found her. Besides, she probably had a bottle somewhere in the room. If not, they could send out for one. The truth was that despite last night's exertions, he was becoming downright horny again. He began to grow hard just from think-

33

ing about her, and he increased the length of his stride in order to get there that little bit quicker.

Sarah did not answer his soft rapping on her door. Could be she was sleeping? If so, he knew a way to wake her. He fingered the buttons of his fly with one hand while with the other he tested the door.

The latch was not set, and the door swung open easily to his touch.

The interior of the small room was nearly dark in the fading light of day, but he could see Sarah stretched out on the bed they'd shared through the previous night. Longarm stepped inside and began unbuttoning his trousers.

A moment later, he turned cold.

He found her lamp and snapped a match aflame to light it. In the yellow glow of lamplight, he could see Sarah. Her flesh was waxy and yellowed, heavily blotched with dark purple bruises over much of her body.

He reached down to touch her and found she was as cold as he now felt. She must have been dead for hours, perhaps since early in the morning.

Longarm felt a surge of fury. The rage that was inside him did not prevent him from moving with gentle care to unfold a blanket to spread over her.

Chapter 8

"You say your name is Harger?"

"That's right, Deputy. John Harger, town marshal of Casper. I am the law here."

Longarm refrained from correcting that statement. Fact was, the law was the law here. Not John Harger. "Are you going to do anything about the murder, Marshal Harger?"

"Told you that I would, didn't I? I've already sent for Jim Willett to fetch the body and bury her. We'll collect her things and sell them at auction. If there's money left over after the burying, we'll use it to buy a memorial marker for her. Whatever her name was."

"I already told you that. Her name is Sarah Osten."

"Fine," the town marshal said, with no show of interest whatsoever. "Write that down. I'll have it put on the memorial if there is one."

"What about the murderer?" Longarm persisted.

Harger shrugged. "She was a whore, Deputy. Whores get beat up all the time. This time the whore happened to die. Happens all the time. You could call it accidental death, really."

"I call it murder," Longarm said.

"Fine. You do that, Deputy. But as it happens, I know as good as you do that murder is not a federal crime. Neither is thumping a whore around."

"Dammit, man, you saw the body. She was deliberately beaten to death."

"If you say so. But it still isn't any of your business, Deputy. This is local. And I am the local law. I'll do what I think best about this. You, Deputy, can just butt out." The town marshal gave him a look of smug self-satisfaction.

"Thank you," Longarm said, his voice heavy with sarcasm. "Thank you ever so fucking much."

"Careful of your mouth, Deputy. We got an ordinance on the books here about public nuisance. Offensive language can fit that, you know. If me and the justice of the peace say that it does."

"I'll keep that in mind, Harger."

"Marshal Harger if you please," the SOB said with a sneer.

Longarm spun on his heels and got the hell out of there before he went and did something Billy Vail would regret.

"Don't be giving me that shit, Goddammit! You know good and well who I'm talking about. That asshole I had trouble with right over there by that table just last night. Now what's his name, and where can I find the son of a bitch?"

"Mister, I don't have any idea what you're talking about," the bartender said with a straight face.

Longarm's bile was commencing to rise. He took a moment to recover control of himself, standing there peering intently at the bar surface instead of into the fat face of the bartender who was lying through his teeth. Longarm stood there in silence and willed his shoulder muscles to let go of the tension that was putting a hump in his back.

When he looked up again, Longarm smiled. The expression was deceptively gentle. Just like his touch with Sarah's body had been.

"What I think," Longarm said calmly, "is that you are interfering with a federal officer in the performance of his duties."

The bartender did not appear to be impressed. "What I think," he said, "is that you have no authority here. Murder is not a federal crime."

"Word goes around this town pretty good, doesn't it?" Longarm observed.

The barman said nothing.

"As it happens," Longarm said, "my investigation has nothing to do with murder. This one is about the fourteenth amendment to the Constitution of the United States. Ever hear of it?"

"Probably, but I don't recall one of those from another. So what about it?"

"So the crime I have in mind would be a violation of that amendment. Which has t' do with involuntary servitude, by the way. You can look that up sometime," Longarm said. "And as a material witness, I have the right to question you."

The bartender looked him in the eye and said, "You just did. I told you I don't remember. Now get out of here. I don't want any more of your business."

Longarm's smile returned. "Mister, you can tell me what I want to know right here and now, or I can put you in manacles and take you on the coach down to Cheyenne and from there on a train to Denver. Put you in a steel cage until your memory returns. And if you don't think I'm willin' to do that, you just feel free t' clamp your mouth closed and stick your wrists out because you and me will be taking a little trip."

"You wouldn't go to all that bother, and I know it."

Longarm sighed. "You called my bluff, didn't you?"

"Yes, I guess I damn sure did."

"Fair enough." Longarm turned and walked away. Down to the far end of the bar. There he flipped open the flattop gate that led into the well behind the bar. He reached into a pocket and brought out a pair of handcuffs that he let dangle loose in his left hand while his right suggestively stroked the butt of his Colt .44. He stepped into the well and approached the bartender.

"Listen, dammit, you aren't gonna. . . ."

"Turn around." Longarm's voice was hard and flat. There was power in the order, and it was probably clear to anyone watching—and every man in the saloon was damned sure watching—that he was in no mood to take any shit. "Do it now."

"Look, I. . . ."

Longarm did not say another word. But one step nearer, and the bartender went suddenly pale. The man turned around and stood there trembling.

"Put your hands behind you."

"Listen, Deputy, I. . . ."

"Do it now."

The bartender pushed his hands behind him. Longarm snapped the manacles into place and squeezed, making sure they were tight enough to bite hard into the man's flesh.

Longarm quickly searched the fellow for weapons, then untied the bartender's apron and dropped it unceremoniously onto the bar. It hit with a solid thump from the weight of coins held in a pocket.

"Look now. . . ."

"Shut up. The only thing I'm willing to listen to out of your mouth is the name and whereabouts of the man who runs the whores around here."

"I . . . Jesus God, mister, he'll be pissed as hell if I say anything to you about this."

"And I'll put your ass in jail if you don't."

"I can't. . . ."

"Suit yourself." Longarm shoved him around to face the open end of the bar well and pushed, sending him tottering on his way with his hands clamped behind his back.

"Jesus, Deputy, I . . . all right. I believe you. I'll tell you. Now . . . please . . . these things hurt something awful."

Longarm stopped the man's forward progress and stood waiting for the information he sought. The cuffs would not be coming off until he knew who the whoremonger was, and where that man could likely be found.

Chapter 9

"Well, well. Funny coincidence finding you here, ain't it?" Longarm said to Marshal John Harger.

Harger was sitting in a straight-backed chair on the porch in front of the law office of Paul Andreson, Esquire. The chair was tipped back so it rested on the back two legs, the top leaning against the office building wall. With Longarm's approach, the marshal leaned forward, dropping the chair back onto all four legs with a loud, dull thump.

"What is your business here, Deputy?" Harger demanded.

Longarm gave him a smile. "None o' yours, that's what."

"You are causing me more trouble than I intend to take from you, mister," the town marshal said. He stood, his right hand held close to the butt of a revolver hanging on his hip.

"I don't get this deal," Longarm said. "Is Andreson paying you off, man? Cash only? Split on the profits? Free pussy whenever you want it? Or some combination of all o' those. What is it with you and him, Harger? An' don't get me wrong here. I'm genuinely interested. It ain't exactly normal for a man in your position t' threaten gunplay over something like this, and I can't figure it out."

"When you come right down to it, Long, that doesn't matter, does it? I've already told you. This is a local matter taking place within my jurisdiction. You have no part in it, and if you overstep your authority, I will be entirely within my rights to call you on it. Right up to and including the use of deadly force if that's where you want to take it. And believe me, Long. I can take you down any time I want."

"I'd rather it didn't come t' that, Harger. An' I got no intention of overstepping my authority. I can promise you that."

"Well now, I am pleased to hear that, Long. Indeed, I am."

"Right." Longarm's lips tightened into something that might have been taken for a smile . . . if the observer was foolish enough to accept it at face value. "You should know, Harger, that I intend to question one of your citizens, identified as a certain Paul Andreson, about possible criminal activity in violation of the Constitution of the United States. That sorta shit is clearly within my jurisdiction, Marshal. And if you've been studying up on these things, you prob'ly already know that in matters like this, federal law supersedes local authority."

"Murder is not. . . ."

"Murder is not what I want to talk t' the man about," Longarm said quietly.

Harger seemed quite taken aback. He looked puzzled, and the air went out of his sails as the tension in his body slacked off. His hand dropped away from the butt of his belly gun.

"You're welcome t' join me inside if you like," Longarm invited.

"Yes, I . . . yes. I will."

41

Harger turned and led the way inside the Casper lawyer's office.

Andreson was the same son of a bitch Longarm had the
run-in with the previous evening. When Harger came in
with Longarm, the lawyer's expression reflected considerable surprise. And no small amount of apprehension.
"What the hell is this, Johnny? Why did you bring this
man inside? I told you I don't want to see him. And I
don't have to. I've already explained that to you ten times,
Johnny. Now take him back out, dammit. Right now."

Harger's mouth worked, but nothing came out for the
moment, as he apparently tried to come up with an explanation.

Longarm took care of that for him. "The marshal is
following the exact letter of the law, Andreson. He's made
it clear to me that he will handle everything that's covered
under the town an' territorial statutes. Naturally, I've
agreed t' that. It's the law. We all three of us understand
that, don't we?"

"Exactly," Andreson puffed. "You have no jurisdiction
here. And I have no interest in talking with you. Now get
out. Johnny, you go, too. Right now, mind. I want nothing
more to do with this."

Longarm sidled to his right a few paces, making no
great show of it, but putting enough distance between
himself and Andreson's desk that he could keep a watch
on both the lawyer and the town marshal without having
to twist around from side to side. He was pretty sure of
Andreson's hostility, less so about Harger, who seemed
to have been defused by Longarm's statements of cooperation.

"Paul Andreson," Longarm intoned with slow deliber-
ation, "it is my duty to inform you that I am placing you
under arrest on federal charges."

Andreson shot to his feet, glaring first at Harger and

then at Longarm. "You son of a bitch, there's nothing about that woman's death that violates federal law."

"I agree with you completely, Counselor," Longarm told him.

"But what . . . ?"

"I am charging you with the involuntary servitude provisions of the United States Constitution, Andreson."

"That is ridiculous. I never once, um, employed French Jenny. Never had anything to do with her. And there is no way you could prove otherwise, damn you. None."

"I'm sure that's right," Longarm agreed. "But then my charge has nothing t' do with Sarah Osten. That was her real name, by th' way. I wouldn't expect you t' know that, but whores have names an' families, too. Which is kinda beside the point. I'm chargin' you with regard t' your other women."

"You have no . . ."

"I have every right, Counselor. I have already placed you under arrest. You'll be taken down t' Denver for arraignment. I'll have warrants issued for your stable o' whores when I get there. You can sit in the pokey an' work up your defense arguments while I come back up here an' hang paper."

Longarm smiled broadly. "What would you think a man would get for that, Counselor? Ten years? Fifteen? An' how d'you think your fellow prisoners would like havin' a lawyer there among 'em? Bet your asshole is three times bigger by the time they spring you outa that prison, Counselor!"

Longarm grinned. "Not that you look all that pretty t' me. But you never know what kinda taste a convict is gonna have after he's been locked away twenty or thirty years. Some o' those boys might find you mighty attractive."

"Johnny, this man is crazy. Get him out of here."

"Paul, I . . . Jesus, Paul. I don't know anything about

this federal shit. You told me . . . Paul, he isn't charging you with any of the stuff you told me about. This is . . . this is different. I don't know what to believe. I just can't . . ."

Harger, who was not being charged with anything, was the one with a look of stricken desperation. Paul Andreson appeared to be angry, but not in the least frightened by this.

"I don't give a shit what I told you before," Andreson barked at his tame marshal. "Now I'm telling you to take him out of here. Do you understand me, Johnny? Get him out. Do whatever you have to do to accomplish that."

"I can't . . . I have to. . . ."

"Turn around, Andreson," Longarm snapped, his voice suddenly hard and cold. "You are under arrest. Put your hands behind your back and stand perfectly still, lest some of us get excited an' do something real stupid.

"Do it *now*!"

Chapter 10

Whatever influence Paul Andreson had on John Harger, however the lawyer held the town marshal in thrall, the force of it must have been unimaginably powerful.

Harger made a noise that was much like a whimper, abrupt and anguished. His hand flashed to the revolver on his hip.

Longarm could scarcely believe that the stupid son of a bitch was doing what he so plainly was indeed doing.

Stupid in more than one way, at that.

John Harger apparently fancied himself one hell of a quick man with a gun.

But then he probably was accustomed to facing half drunk cowboys on Saturday nights.

Custis Long did not fit into that category. Hardly.

Longarm did not even have to think about it. He pulled his double-action Colt and triggered a shot before Harger came close to cocking his pistol. That bullet slammed into Harger's side just beneath his ribs. Casper's town marshal went suddenly pale, his face going loose and limp, a sure indication that the wound was a mortal one.

Longarm did not waste any time contemplating Harger's condition. He immediately leaped to the side, with-

45

out even bothering to look toward Andreson to see what he was up to.

Longarm's attention returned to the lawyer in time to see the man's hand come out of the top drawer of his desk. Andreson had a pistol in his fist and obviously no reluctance about using it on a federal peace officer.

Likely he thought—if he took time enough to think about the situation at all—that he could lie his way out of this. Whether John Harger was alive to swear to Andreson's story or not, if Longarm was dead, so was any threat of prison time for Paul Andreson. Once Longarm was gone, Andreson could build a pile of plausible lies deep enough to hide any number of sins.

If Longarm was dead, that is.

Andreson's impulse to reach for the gun while Longarm was busy with Harger proved to be his last.

Longarm fired and a blunt tipped .44-40 slug ripped into Andreson's chest through the hard cartilage of his breastbone.

The man staggered, but remained on his feet so Longarm fired again, taking more careful aim this time. The bullet struck just left of the bridge of Andreson's nose. A halolike red spray appeared behind Andreson's head, and both blood and bits of gray brain tissue liberally splattered the wallpaper behind him.

Longarm turned away from the already dead Andreson and once more swung the muzzle of his Colt toward Harger.

By now, the lawman was down, stretched out on the floor with one hand placed over the wound in his side, as if that would somehow make this all go away.

There was very little blood in evidence. The bullet must have churned around inside Harger without ever exiting, the most damaging form of gunshot possible. The man's body had absorbed all the wicked energy in that slug, and his insides probably looked like they'd been through a

46

meat grinder, even though virtually no blood was leaking from the entry wound.

Harger was still alive, but he had no interest at all in trying to shoot Longarm now. His revolver lay forgotten on the lawyer's office floor. Longarm walked over to Harger and took a moment to kick the gun—it was an engraved and nickel-plated single-action Colt, he saw now—and send it skittering across the floor to end up against the wall. Only when that was well out of reach did he holster his own Colt and hunker down beside the dying man.

"You've killed me, haven't you?" Harger asked, his voice a thin whisper.

"Yes, I expect that I have, Marshal." It was plain from the man's ashen complexion and slack features that he was on his way out. The only amazement was that he was not yet dead.

"Marshal," Harger repeated. His lips fluttered. He seemed to be trying to smile. "I was . . . time was, I was a good marshal."

"I believe you, Harger," Longarm said in a strong, crisp voice. The words were a lie, of course. John Harger never saw the day when he deserved the respect that ought to be attached to a badge.

But what the fuck. The man was dying. Longarm saw no need to send him into eternity with the condemnation of a peer as his final memory.

Harger gasped for breath. It was obvious he had little left. He lay there for a moment with his mouth opening and closing, much like a fish freshly caught and thrown onto the bank.

"Long," he managed.

"Yes, Marshal?"

"Tell my wife . . . tell her . . ."

Longarm never learned what Harger wanted his wife to know. The man died before he could get the words out.

47

The spark of life was extinguished from his eyes, and his body collapsed into itself like a rubber pillow with the air let out of it.

Funny, Longarm thought, how a man becomes smaller in death.

He stood and reached into his coat pocket for a handful of blunt, stubby .44-40 cartridges so he could reload the Colt before going on to anything else.

He would look up the widow this evening, he figured. That would be the least he could do. And what the hell. He would tell her that Harger died assisting Longarm with the apprehension of Paul Andreson. The town would likely make a hero out of the pissant son of a bitch.

He would tell the grieving widow that her husband's last thoughts were about her. And he would tell her Harger's last words were that he loved her.

Longarm figured he'd caused this woman enough grief already. No point in adding salt to her wounds now.

He looked around at the bloody carnage that was in this room now and shook his head.

It'd been so useless. So unnecessary.

The good news—if that's what it was—was that Sarah Osten's murderer had been brought to account.

And now maybe Casper would have itself a better man for its town marshal.

Longarm went out onto the street so he could ask someone how he might find the widow Harger.

Chapter 11

The stagecoach made a brief stop in Buffalo—which Longarm always thought to be one of the prettiest towns anywhere, what with the tidy homes and creek running through and the Big Horn mountains looming to the west—then rolled onward toward Cade's Station.

Cade's had been there even before the coach line was established, first as a trading post and later as a way station on the old Bozeman Trail. The place looked like some huge hand gathered up a collection of mismatched, falling-apart sheds and shacks and shanties and tossed them willy-nilly onto the ground like dice being thrown.

The oldest structures were dugouts carved into a hillside and roofed with sod. There were also some truly ratty looking log buildings made from aspen. Which accounted for their unsightly appearance. Aspen is easily cut and easy to haul, but no power on earth will keep it from warping out of true once laid in place, so anything built with it soon comes to look like it is made not of timber but of straw.

The long, low main building, which housed Charlie Boyd's store and the eatery where coach passengers could fill up, was originally a soddy, made using squares of prairie sod like building blocks and roofed with more of the same. This one in later years was faced with aspen saplings set vertically against the walls and then laced with willow withes, then the whole thing plastered over with a mud and grass mortar. The place was ugly but sturdy.

An assortment of corrals, sheds and small shanties were scattered nearby, offering shelter to the coach line's relay livestock, flat-faced Indian whores, wolf trappers or the occasional passerby wanting a roof over his head for a night or two.

The crowning glory at Cade's was the owner's mansion. Not that it was all that much as mansions went, but for a place like Cade's it was pretty grand. It was a house—a genuine, honest-to-God house—with stone walls and a split shingle roof and a front porch where the proprietor could sit and contemplate his domain. For the last three or four years, that man was Charlie Boyd. Or so the man called himself now. Boyd's past was a never mentioned mystery and likely he'd been known by other names in other places. He seemed a decent enough sort, however, and Longarm had no interest in prying into Boyd's past. Longarm'd had a casual acquaintance with him for about two years or a trifle longer. He wouldn't say that he especially liked Boyd, but certainly did not dislike him.

Longarm crawled down out of the stagecoach along with the other northbound passengers. Unlike them, he untied the canvas cover on the luggage boot and fetched down his carpetbag and the old McClellan saddle with his rifle scabbard strapped to it. He nodded a thank-you to the jehu and his assistant, then carried his gear inside the store building.

Boyd was behind the counter, perched atop a tall stool like a buzzard waiting for something dead to show up. The coach passengers were already seated and were being treated to the prairie dog stew that was the staple diet at Cade's.

Boyd eyed Longarm's bag and saddle and observed, "I see you've come prepared to stay a spell, Marshal."

"That's right." Longarm set his things down and reached for a cheroot. He offered one to Boyd as well, but the man declined.

"I'm a man without vices," Boyd said when he passed on the offer. Then he laughed. So did Longarm. Charlie Boyd neither smoked nor drank—Longarm suspected he might be Mormon—but he was practically legendary when it came to other forms of debauchery. Longarm attributed most of the stories told about Boyd to plain old gossip run rampant, or to outright jealousy. It was said the man could service half a dozen of his Indian bawds at a time and throw in a Mexican or two if one was handy. They said he could do this night after night if there wasn't enough business to keep his whores gainfully occupied with paying customers. But that was only hearsay. Longarm hadn't personally observed him doing it, of course. And had no damn desire to do so.

"When will the next westbound come through?" Longarm asked.

"You figure to stay here until then?" Boyd countered.

"I do."

"Government voucher for your room and board?"

Longarm nodded. "That's right."

Boyd grinned. "Good! That guarantees me a good profit for the year."

"How's that?" Longarm asked with one eyebrow raised.

"Last coach I seen roll west from here was last . . . I dunno, Marshal. Last winter some time, I think it was."

"Pardon me? I thought there was a stagecoach line running east and west into Crawford County now. The Hysop Express Company they told me it was."

Boyd shrugged. "Could be for all I know. 'Bout the

51

only thing I can tell you, Marshal, is that there is an ambulance fitted out for passengers like a mud wagon, and it does come out from Crawford and go back in again. It was busy as hell last summer. But only carrying people *into* Crawford. It only brought anybody out, oh, a half dozen times maybe. Then took them back a week or so after. They went south from here and came back the same way o' course." He paused.

"You want to know something really funny, Marshal? They all of them, all but maybe three, they all of them was women."

"*Women*? The whole damned bunch of them?"

"That's what I'm telling you, Marshal, an' while I might lie to you about some things, I got no reason to make that one up. Bunch of females. Middle-aged mostly, hard looking old battle-axes. Looked like they ought to belong to some temperance league or like that. 'Course you know me. I never met a woman that wasn't pretty once you throw her skirts up over her face. But this bunch . . . they're cold. Never got a one of them to show a smile, much less a petticoat."

"I'll be damned," Longarm mumbled. "And that's all the traffic there has been in and out on the eastwest road?"

"Now, that isn't exactly what I said, Marshal. Said that's the only time I seen that coach, if coach is what it be. I've seen some freight wagons go over there full and come back empty. Seen quite a bunch of those. There's a funny thing about that, too. The drivers of those rigs generally stopped here on their way in. Not a one of them stopped back again on his way out. Just came out on the road and turned north from here."

"North," Longarm repeated.

"That's right. They'd generally come outa the east, go on into Crawford County, and then turn north once they was running empty. Drove past at night, some of them. Right on past. I could hear from the way they rattled though that those wagon beds was empty. It's a puzzlement, I tell you."

"I expect that it is," Longarm agreed. "So you don't know anything about a coach line called Hysop."

"Nope. Not a thing."

"What about mail bags? Have you seen any mail bags go in or out?"

"Never," Boyd said. "I handle mail all the time. I know a mail bag when I see one. I haven't seen any from that direction."

"What about a town called Harrisonville?"

Boyd shook his head. "Never heard of it."

"I'll be damned," Longarm said.

Boyd grinned. "That could well be, Marshal, but it's a subject I won't speculate about. I got enough on my own plate to handle." He laughed. "Even though I'm a man without vices."

"Yes, of course you are."

"You still want to stay?" Boyd asked.

"I do. But maybe not until the next stagecoach going that way. I'll want a room—no, don't bother t' ask; I won't be wanting company along with the room, thank-you—and a horse. You got a horse I can hire?"

"Marshal, I got just damn near anything you could want if you're willing to pay me for it."

Longarm believed him, but did not have any desire to prove the claim.

"Everything on voucher?"

"That's right. This is all official." With many men Longarm would have offered a reminder that the government rates are not flexible and that he would personally be checking to make sure there were no overcharges. Of course, he hated doing dull and dreary paperwork, and seldom bothered, but businessmen in the far-flung towns deputies visited wouldn't know that. But Charlie Boyd had always been scrupulously honest in his billing in the past. Longarm figured he likely would be still.

"You hungry, Marshal?"

"Enough t' eat horse."

"Marshal, if that's what you want . . ." Boyd spread his hands and gave Longarm a look of mock innocence. Then, he said, "If you can wait ten minutes until those sheep are outa here, I'll have them serve you up something better than squirrel stew."

"Charlie, where in hell would you find a squirrel in these parts?"

Boyd's grin was unabashed. "That's what I'm calling it nowadays. Sounds ever so much better than prairie dog, doesn't it? And some professor looking fella passing through told me that squirrels and prairie dogs are related, so it isn't really a lie."

Longarm shook his head, but had to chuckle. "Charlie, prairie dogs aren't related to squirrels. That fella must've been thinking about the little short tail ground squirrels they got up in the mountains. Folks up there that don't know better call those prairie dogs, but they aren't. Down here you got the real thing, an' they look to me like they're kin to the woodchucks we had back where I come from. I used to shoot them when I was a boy, and they even taste pretty much the same as prairie dog."

"Really." The man looked sad. "Guess I'll have to think about that some."

"If it makes you feel any better, it was a professor that told you they're big-ass squirrels. He'd know a lot more than me."

Boyd brightened. "Yeah. That's right. Maybe I can go on calling it squirrel stew after all."

"You do that," Longarm said.

"Tell you what. Wait until the sheep have ate and gone, and I'll have my women fix you up a nice elk steak and some rice and gravy. How's that sound?"

"A helluva lot better than squirrel stew. How's about

54

pouring me a drink for while I'm waiting?"

"You want the good stuff, as I recall." Good, of course, was a relative term. But then Cade's Station under Charlie Boyd's management was known for its vile but potent Injun whiskey as much as for its prairie dog stew. Longarm knew better than to put any of that nasty stuff into his belly. Well, unless there was nothing else available, of course.

"I'll have the bottled-in-bond, please."

"For you, Marshal, I'll even pour it into a cup that doesn't have any paraffin in the bottom."

Longarm wasn't sure if the man was serious about that or not. But in a tin cup, paraffin went unseen and was often used to fill a portion of the vessel so a man would think he was being given more than was actually poured. It was an old trick, and a common one, but most men never seemed to catch onto it.

"Go ahead and sit down. We'll take care of you. Just leave your things if you like. It won't be bothered."

Longarm nodded and walked over to the common area where the stagecoach passengers were hurriedly gulping their stew before the driver roared for them to load up or be left behind . . . a threat that was entirely sincere in most instances.

He sat down, and while he waited he wondered just what in hell was going on at this Harrisonville place if even Charlie Boyd did not know anything about it.

Chapter 12

The horse Charlie Boyd rented to him was an ugly SOB, but it had large nostrils and a deep chest cavity and front legs set wide apart, so it probably had staying power to spare. On the downside, its shoulder blades lay nearly vertical beneath the skin, so its trot would be harsh enough to chip a man's teeth and rattle his brains. A nice forty-five degree angle is what you want to see in that shoulder bone.

It also had a short-bobbed tail but long mane, so he suspected Boyd must have gotten it from some passing Indians. Sure enough, when he approached the animal with his saddle, it became nervous and tried to sidle away from him with plenty of white around the eyes, showing its fear. It shook its head and snorted in alarm, but did not fight the rope that held it tied to a fence post. Looked ready to booger though.

Longarm stopped where he was and peered at the animal while he took out a cheroot and lighted it, giving the horse time to calm down a mite. Then, he picked up the saddle and walked around to the off side of the horse, instead. The animal was relaxed and calm when he approached it from the right side where Indians habitually mounted.

"No problem there, old son," Longarm muttered reassuringly while he saddled the horse and stroked it a little. "I'll try an' remember t' do things your way."

Longarm's own preference was that a horse should be accustomed to being mounted from either side. That wasn't so important down here in flat country, but in the mountains a man just naturally wanted to get on or off by way of whichever side happened to be uphill. It could be a real bitch trying to dismount downhill if the horse was standing sideways on a steep slope.

But this wasn't his horse to worry about training, and hopefully it wouldn't matter that it only liked to be approached from the right-hand side.

Longarm finished gearing up and tied his carpetbag behind the cantle of the old McClellan. His belly was warm and full after a breakfast of oat porridge and hot coffee, and the newly breaking day looked fine as fine might be.

He stepped onto the horse and reined it west along the faintly visible tracks of what passed for a road out here.

Sundown found him short of Harrisonville, but apparently close enough to spit at it. A couple miles or so west he could see smoke rising from the far side of a low hogback. Must be Harrisonville, he figured. And it seemed silly to stop and make a camp when he could hire a bed for the night just that little bit ahead.

The Indian horse shook its head and pawed at the ground impatiently while Longarm sat pondering whether to ride straight to the smoke or swing around the south end of the small hill so as to avoid having to climb up and over. The hell with it. The horse hadn't yet thought about breaking a sweat after a full day of alternating its long-striding smooth road walk with a rocking chair lope—he hadn't yet tried its trot and didn't damn well intend to—and obviously had strength enough to handle most anything. He'd just go straight to the smoke and not fret about the climbing.

Longarm lighted himself another cheroot—that distant smoke put the notion in mind—and bumped the horse into a lope.

When he breasted the crest of the hogback an hour or so later, the horse still felt strong beneath him. He stopped at the top to let it blow a little while he looked with some surprise at what he could see down below.

If there was a town there, it was one that went to sleep almighty early. He could see only two glimmers of lamplight from the place where that smoke had been rising. The moon wouldn't be up for several more hours, but there was starlight enough that he could make out several dark shapes that would be buildings. Only two of those, one fairly large, showed lamps burning.

There was no noise reaching him. No sound save the whisper of a night breeze rustling softly in the tall grass close by. No piano playing. No laughter. No singing. Nothing.

Strange, he thought. Still, strange or not, he was here. Best to get on with what needed doing.

He leaned back in his saddle and nudged the horse into a slow, hip-swaying downhill walk.

No damn wonder he hadn't heard piano music or laughter. This was no town he'd reached. As he came near he could see that what he'd assumed to be Harrisonville was instead a ranch layout.

The large building with lights showing from its windows was a house, undoubtedly that of the owner, while the other long low structure with lights would be the bunkhouse.

Longarm reined toward the owner's place and stopped in front of the steps leading up to a front porch that ran the entire width of the place. A couple rocking chairs, empty at the moment, were placed there.

"Hello, the house. Hello."

He had to call several times before anyone responded. A fat woman wearing an apron came out. She greeted him in a language he did not understand—it was not Spanish or Lakota or any other language that he might at least have recognized—then tried again in heavily accented English. "Who you, meestair?"

Longarm removed his hat and held it down by his belly. "I'm a passing stranger, ma'am, looking for a meal an' a place t' sleep." He wasn't sure just how much of that she might understand, but she nodded and told him; "You wai' heah now," and disappeared inside the house.

A minute later she was back. She pointed toward what he assumed was the bunkhouse and said, "You go there, meestair. Tell them meestair say." She didn't mention what mister nor what it was that "meestair" said Longarm was to say. That was all right. He had permission to step down and stay the night. That was what mattered.

He thanked her and reined away toward the bunkhouse.

Chapter 13

"HH Connected," the *segundo*, a gent named Martin, told him. "American owners, too, not English. There's an awful lot of limeys coming into this country lately, but Henry Harrison is as American as you or me. He's building himself quite a spread here. Still expanding. Still looking for hands." Martin looked him over and said, "You don't look like any out-of-work cowhand, but if you happen to be looking for a job, I'd be glad to put a word in for you."

"Thanks," Longarm said, "but I'm not interested. Mighty kind of you to suggest it, though."

"Yeah, well, if you change your mind."

"Sure. Thanks." No one had mentioned food, and Longarm hadn't stopped to make himself a supper after spotting the smoke he'd assumed marked Harrisonville. Which, now that he thought about it, was almost certainly named for the owner of the HH Connected. In any event, his stomach was rumbling. It wouldn't have been polite to ask to be fed, of course. It looked like he would just have to go to sleep hungry. He hadn't thought to pack any jerky or other ready-to-eat grub. Dammit.

"What is it that brings you this way, if you aren't looking for work?" Martin asked in an offhand tone. He wasn't trying to pry, Longarm thought, merely making friendly conversation while Longarm was busy spreading his blanket on the wooden slat bunk provided by the HH Connected. Several of the other bunks were occupied by snoring cowboys, while down at the far end of the long, open room there was a card game in progress.

There was no reason to hide his identity here. This job was certainly nothing to get excited about, and he'd already looked over the HH Connected hands to see there was no one in the building he recognized as being wanted. Still, a natural caution kept him from being too open about the specifics of the job.

"Deputy U.S. marshal," was all he said, "just passing through on my way to some place called Harrisonville. I'm hoping come daybreak you can direct me to it."

"Sure thing. Harrisonville, that's just about eight miles from here." Martin hesitated for a moment, then his curiosity got the best of him. "If you don't mind me asking, who is it you're after in Harrisonville?"

Longarm laughed. "Nobody. I'm not after nobody, friend. Just gathering information, that's all. The job ain't all excitement and gun smoke, y'know. Mostly it's tedious an' boring an' dull." He grinned. "Kind of like punching cows if I remember correctly."

"Thought you looked like you might know one end of a cow from the other."

Longarm shrugged. "That was a long time ago. I've forgot a lot since then. Let's see now. You raise the critters for milk an' cheese, is that it?" He'd never seen a longhorn bovine that would stand still for being milked nor give more than a few gills at a time if ever it was wrestled down and forced to give up its milk. And Martin wouldn't have either.

The HH Connected *segundo* chuckled and moved toward the table where some of the boys were playing cards. "See you in the morning, Marshal."

61

Longarm nodded and sat on the end of the bunk to pull his boots off. Martin passed by the card table and went outside.

It wasn't terribly late, but the HH Connected hands hadn't seemed especially welcoming, and Longarm had no desire to intrude on a card game that looked to be a private affair, so it looked like he would get an early sleep for a change. He'd carefully folded his coat and put it onto a shelf and was unbuttoning his shirt when Martin returned.

"Say now, Marshal, I clean forgot that you might be hungry. Sorry I didn't think of it before, but I tell you what. I've kicked the cook outa his bed and told him we got a visitor that needs some supper. He's cooking you a steak and boiling some fresh coffee right now. You want to come with me, I'll show you to the slop trough that passes for a chuck hall here."

Longarm was surprised. Truth to tell, his curiosity was piqued as well. It was normal enough for a late arriving visitor to be offered whatever was left over from the hands's supper. But to get a cook to fry steak and make a fresh pot of coffee after he'd already cleaned up his kitchen and pulled his fires? Now that was not exactly usual.

Still and all, Longarm started redoing the shirt buttons.

He hesitated for half a second or so when it came to picking up his gunbelt. That wouldn't be considered a very friendly gesture.

But then no gun is worth a tinker's damn if it's elsewhere when it's needed. He strapped the Colt on again before he followed Martin out into the night.

"Marshal, this is Henry Harrison, the gentleman who owns the HH Connected," Martin said, introducing a tall, handsome man with gray showing at his temples, steel gray eyes and flecks of gray visible also in his mustache and carefully groomed goatee. When he smiled and extended his hand to shake, Harrison looked like he had teeth enough for two men and every one of them dazzling white. He wore a sure-enough gentleman's smoking jacket complete with satin lapels, silk britches and soft, low cut shoes that looked like they'd never before this night ventured off carpet.

"What a pleasure it is to have a celebrity in our midst," Harrison said as he pumped Longarm's hand and smiled and smiled and smiled.

"No celebrity," Longarm said. "Just a working fella passing through."

"Even so, Deputy, we are honored to have you here. Really. What did you say your name is?"

"Custis Long. Out of U.S. Marshal William Vail's office down in Denver," he said, neglecting for no particular reason to invite the brilliantly-smiling rancher to use his nickname instead.

"Long. Custis Long." Harrison pursed his lips and thought for a moment. "Ah, yes. I believe I've heard of you. They say you are a good man, Deputy. Very fair, I am told."

"I try t' be, sir."

"And I am sure you succeed. Martin, tell Chubby we want Deputy Long to have only the best."

"Yes, sir." Martin disappeared into the kitchen, where Longarm could hear loud rattling and banging of the sort that hinted rather broadly at the presence of a very unhappy cook. Chubby, he guessed, did not much appreciate being dragged out of bed to cook for some stranger.

Harrison was still smiling. "I wish I'd known who you are to begin with, Deputy. I would have brought you into my house instead of asking you to stay with the hands and eat in the cookhouse."

"I don't want t' be a bother, sir."

"No bother. Truly. It is our pleasure to help you gentlemen who are charged with keeping the peace in this vast land. Please consider yourself welcome here at any time, Deputy. I mean that sincerely."

"Thank you, sir."

"Sit down. Please. Join me for coffee while your supper is being prepared." There was already a pot placed at one end of the table along with a stack of heavy ceramic cups, a dish of pale brown sugar and a freshly opened can of evaporated milk. "Please."

Longarm sat where Harrison pointed, and the rancher took a chair opposite him. "What is it that brings you so far out from civilization, Deputy?"

"Oh, nothing at all important, Mr. Harrison. Just kind of getting acquainted really. There's been so many changes around here that my boss thought we ought to know what's up here, if you see what I mean. There's not been any crime reported here. None at all. And I'm not looking to arrest anybody or serve any papers, nothing like that. Just taking a look-see. That's all."

"Very sensible of your marshal, I'm sure," Harrison said as he stirred generous portions of both milk and sugar into his coffee. "It pays to be prepared in advance of any difficulties. I am a great believer in that myself."

"Yes, sir, that's the way the marshal sees things, too."

"Good man, this Vail. I've heard excellent things about him. Not political as I understand it. A true lawman."

"Yes, sir, he is that."

"Excellent. Excellent," Harrison said.

Chubby pushed his way through a swinging door that separated the kitchen from the chuck hall, both hands full with a huge tray. The cook—who was as lean as a bull-whip—wore a very carefully neutral expression despite the clanging and grumbling that had been going on when the door was closed.

The tray held enough food for five men. There was an assortment of thick steaks ribbed with crisp fat, potatoes both fried and mashed, thick, brown gravy, English peas fresh from someone's garden, biscuits so fluffy they looked like they might float off their plate and end up against the ceiling, even a crock of bright yellow butter. You didn't see butter on just every ranch cookhouse table. Nor fresh garden produce either, for that matter. Longarm guessed they damn sure were offering him their best.

Which inevitably raised the question . . . *why?* Why in hell would Henry Harrison go and do something like that?

Longarm had no idea what the answer to that might be. But he did know he was hungry enough to eat the tray all this good stuff rested on, and that was all he really needed to know right at this moment.

He quit worrying about nonessentials and got busy surrounding the meal Chubby had put together for him.

Chapter 14

Wondering what Henry Harrison was up to gnawed at Longarm right on through to breakfast, which he ate in the cookhouse with the hands even though he was invited into the boss's house. He declined the offer, saying he wanted to get an early start and not wait until folks in the main house stirred. The truth was that he figured he had more chance of getting some answers if he ate with the hands.

And he did, in a manner of speaking.

What he discovered was that Henry Harrison, whatever else he might be up to, most definitely was *not* intent on taking what was not his by force. The HH Connected cowhands were no collection of gun carrying hard cases. Far from it.

For the most part, these cowboys really were boys. Most of them likely hadn't yet seen their twentieth birthdays, and two of them looked like they never yet found need for a razor.

There wasn't a firearm in evidence among them. Nor, Longarm noticed, did any of them have any shiny spots on their trousers put there by the everyday wearing of a holster. A man who looks closely at what is in front of him can see things beyond the obvious, and any lawman worth his salt soon learns to look for those things. Longarm found no signs here of anything but a bunch of sleepy, happy, horseplaying cowboys getting ready for another day of work.

The *segundo* Martin sat at the foot of the long table while the foreman, a short and stocky man named Billingsley occupied the head of the table. Obviously Henry Harrison was not accustomed to entering the cookhouse else that spot would have been reserved for him.

Billingsley stood no more than five foot four or five and at first glance looked like a sawed-off fat man. He was about as wide as he was tall and had a round, moon face and large, pale blue eyes. He looked like a jolly sort but nothing special. That impression quickly faded once he moved. Despite his shape, the HH Connected foreman moved like an athlete. Or, Longarm thought, a circus strongman, which seemed closer to the truth.

He was broad, but a second or third look at him revealed there wasn't any fat included. That heft was all muscle. Short as he was, Longarm would not want to get into a wrestling match with him. Likely Billingsley threw calves for branding by picking them up and putting them down where he wanted them.

He seemed to know his job, too. The laughing, playful, elbow-poking cowboys put their morning hijinks aside and got dead quiet the moment Billingsley cleared his throat and peered down the table at them.

The youngsters bowed their heads and put their hands in their laps, and Billingsley muttered a brief, swift prayer. Then, as the hands grabbed for the bowls of porridge and platters of hotcakes Chubby already had in place, Billingsley began telling off work assignments for the day. Chuck and Carlos out to Pilgrim's Knob—wherever that was—to chouse strays out of the brush and bring them out to the herd so they wouldn't get the idea they could live as free spirits forever. Tex and Dinkins riding the bogs to pull loose any beeves that managed to get themselves belly down in the mud. Lewis and . . . the orders went on like that while the boys stuffed themselves with huge quantities of hot food. Of course they were young and active and wouldn't have a chance to eat again until nightfall. Even so, Longarm was amazed by how much grub some of those skinny kids could pack away. And in practically no time at all.

Chouse. The word stuck out in Longarm's hearing. It was a word common down in Arizona, less so elsewhere. Not that it mattered where Billingsley came from. Longarm wondered if Harrison had come up from the south, also.

The foreman ignored Longarm until the hands were fed and the day's orders given, then he leaned back and acknowledged the deputy's presence with a nod. "Have enough to eat, Marshal?"

"I'm fine, thanks."

"If there's anything you need, just ask. The boss said you're to be treated as his own personal guest."

"Don't need a thing, but I thank you for offering."

"He said you're on your way to Harrisonville."

"That's right. Care for a cheroot?"

"No, thank you, and we don't allow smoking inside the cookhouse."

"All right. Sorry." Longarm laid the unlighted cigar down beside his plate, careful to avoid a spill of sorghum syrup deposited on the table by one of the more boisterous cowhands.

"There's a road of sorts. You likely saw it yesterday on your way here," Billingsley said.

"I followed it out from Cade's Station."

"Right, well, you just keep on it straight west another eight or nine miles. I expect you'll recognize it when you see it."

"I expect so," Longarm agreed.

Billingsley nodded. He paused for a moment, cleared his throat, peered down at his coffee cup—either he'd already eaten in his own quarters or was waiting until everyone else was gone, because even though he had a plate in front of him, he hadn't yet put so much as a spoonful of anything onto it—then he said, "Mind a word of advice?"

"I'd be grateful," Longarm said. He meant it. Billingsley knew the lay of things around here. And by that Longarm meant much more than just the slope of the ground. He was always willing to pay attention to someone who knew what he was talking about, and he suspected that this Roger Billingsley had more than muscle between his ears.

"When you get to Harrisonville . . . don't be too quick to judge."

Longarm gave him a sharp, questioning look.

"Not the sort of judgment you do as a deputy marshal. That isn't the sort of thing I mean. You won't find a more law-abiding group than those people over at Harrisonville. It's just . . . please, don't judge them. That's all."

"Care to explain that any further?" Longarm asked.

Billingsley pondered the question for a moment, then shook his head. "No, I don't think so. Just remember what I said. When you get there. You know?"

"Not yet, I don't. But I expect that I will. And I will keep your advice in mind when I do. That's a promise."

Billingsley looked relieved. "They're nice folks once you get to know them," he said.

"I'll remember that, too, thank you."

The foreman cleared his throat and looked vaguely uncomfortable. Longarm stood and picked up the cheroot he was wanting to light. "Please express my thanks once again to Mr. Harrison, will you?"

Billingsley nodded. "You come by any time, Deputy.

69

You'll always find a meal here or a bed, anything you need."

Longarm told the foreman good-bye and went out to find his horse and get on down the road to this Harrison-ville—where the folks were nice once you got to know them, and where he oughtn't to form any hasty judgments. Whatever all that was supposed to mean.

He stopped immediately outside the cookhouse door to snap a lucifer afire and bend the tip of his cheroot to it, then ambled on his way.

Chapter 15

The wood hadn't yet had time to weather gray on the buildings of Harrisonville. The stores and houses were uniform as to construction and materials, all of them put together in plain, boxy shapes with lumber that had been cut, milled and cured somewhere far from Harrisonville. Longarm could be certain of that because trees were in short supply down here in the broad basin that made up most of Crawford County. There were forested mountains to the south and the west and cedar-dappled hills to the north, but here in the middle of the basin there was only grass.

And water. Harrisonville was built at the confluence of three streams, the largest flowing out of the west, a smaller creek coming up from the south and a small rill coming off the hills to the north.

A dam had been built—none too long ago judging by the ground cover that had been planted to help stabilize the earthen structure—to provide an impoundment of at least a half section in size. Irrigation ditches radiated out from the dam like spokes on a wheel, each of them with control gates at the reservoir and more of the wooden boxes placed to control the flow of irrigation water at the many finger ditches that came off those primary ditches.

Most of the ditches, like most of the small farm parcels they were designed to serve, appeared to be fallow. Not enough people to use them all, Longarm figured. There seemed to be more fields available than houses to populate them. The city fathers of Harrisonville were quite obviously planning ahead to the future.

But then the whole shebang, including the town streets, had a look of careful planning and diligent effort, especially considering how new it all was.

The town itself had streets laid out in checkerboard squares, the streets scraped bare of grass but not surfaced. There were, he noticed as he rode in, no wheel ruts visible on the streets of Harrisonville.

The only ruts he saw were on the two streets that ran parallel to the main business street, one block off of it to either side so they ran directly behind the line of storefronts. Longarm considered how that could be, and the only reasonable conclusion he could come up with was that wagons were used here purely for the purposes of delivering heavy goods to the stores.

Everything else must be by horse or . . .

He stopped. Frowned for a moment and stood in his stirrups to get a better look around.

There were no horses in evidence here. None. No saddle horses. No draft horses. Not even any corrals or small stables adjacent to any of the residences.

Down at the far end of the town there was what looked to be a walled enclosure and loafing shed. If any horses were housed there he could not see them from the east end of town.

That was just about the damnedest thing he'd come across in a long while. The folk in Harrisonville *walked* everywhere? *Farmed* without horses? Be damned.

No wonder Roger Billingsley warned him about being quick to judge.

72

Nice folks, Billingsley said. Once you got to know them.

What the man did not say was that these people were so . . . different.

Well, everybody is entitled to his own way of doing, Longarm figured. Including these odd people here in Harrisonville.

Maybe it was some sort of religious thing with them. Maybe they . . .

He reined the horse to a stop at the edge of town and frowned again as he looked at the street that lay before him.

There were two things that seemed to be conspicuous in their absence now that he got to thinking about it. No, three. And for a town as carefully planned as Harrisonville, he kind of wondered why.

There was no church. There was no school. And—craziest thing of all—there were no saloons or beer parlors anywhere in sight.

Weird.

But none of this would be for religious reasons since there wasn't any church. A religious colony—and he'd seen a number of those over the years—could be expected to build its church before it built anything else. That sure wasn't the case here at Harrisonville.

It was still fairly early when Longarm reached the town, having made his start from the HH Connected just as day was breaking, and the ride being but an hour's easy canter away. Harrisonville was commencing to come to life for the day.

Off to either side he could see people walking out to their farms. Shop doors swinging open. Pedestrians beginning to appear on the street carrying baskets over their arms. The usual flow of a town beginning its day.

Except . . . there were no children, he observed. And no dogs. No rattle of wagon wheels.

He noticed that the farmers were walking in bunches of two or three together, generally with at least one in each group of them pulling hand carts loaded with small implements that were too far away for him to make out. So apparently they did do their farming without the help of horses. No wonder then the plots were small, little more than a decent home garden would be.

At this distance and this early in the planting season, Wyoming being so late to give up its winter, he could not make out what sort of crops were being grown here. And . . . damn. Now there was another thing he didn't see in Harrisonville. Not only were there no horses, there seemed to be no other form of livestock, either. No hogs, chickens, geese, guinea fowl, sheep, goats—none of the creatures generally kept to produce meat and eggs. What the hell kind of farmer didn't raise his own meat?

Nice folks, he reminded himself. Don't judge them too early. Get to know them first. And thank you, Mr. Billingsley for that excellent advice.

The next logical step, Longarm figured, would therefore be to get to know them. A little. Just long enough, really, to stop by the post office and see did it really exist. Then he could smile and nod and shake a few hands and get the hell back to Denver where maybe Billy Vail would have something interesting for him to do.

He kneed the horse forward and entered the main street of Harrisonville at a slow walk.

Chapter 16

There were no horses in Harrisonville. Nor any hitching rail either, he discovered when he stepped down to the ground and looked around for something solid to tie to. That was reasonable enough, he supposed. He just hadn't thought about such an outlandish possibility as living without horses and the means to care for them.

If he'd known this particular horse well enough to be sure of how it would act, he could have just taken a wrap around one of the vertical supports holding up a porch roof. But he did not know the horse that well, and allowing his mount to go larruping off down the street with half a roof flopping and bouncing behind it—probably not an ideal way to introduce himself to the good folk of the community.

Longarm led the animal fruitlessly down the street for several blocks without finding anything he could trust to tie it to, pausing every few paces to nod and tip his hat to ladies passing on the board sidewalks in front of the stores. Eventually he realized he was not likely to find what he needed and took a side street to the wagon road that paralleled the pedestrian avenue.

Sure enough. He found a hitching block there. Not a

rail of the sort intended for saddle horses but a block of sandstone with an iron ring affixed to it. Longarm took the picket rope off his saddle and used that to securely tie the horse. He would worry about feed and water later. But he already suspected that would mean taking the horse well clear of the town limits and staking it out on the native grass.

He went back to the street and looked for signs to tell him what each business was.

There were none. Not a single sign in evidence. Everyone who lived here probably already knew which stores offered what goods. It seemed they were not concerned with the convenience of passersby.

Given a normal community—which Harrisonville was decidedly not—he would have made the barbershop his first stop, so he could get a shave before getting down to business.

Here, he had no idea which of the twenty or so shops in town would house the barber. There had to be one. Every town has at least one barber. But here, there was no red and white spiral post in evidence to point the way for him.

With a half-contained sigh, Longarm stepped up onto the boardwalk and entered the largest shop on the block where he happened to be standing. The place was a mercantile, he quickly saw. It seemed to specialize in ladies wear and accessories. There were buttons and needles, thread and papers of pins. Wide-brimmed hats with artificial flowers sewn where a man's hatband would have been. Scarves and shawls. Shoes and button hooks. Bolts of cloth and headache powders.

Several women were in the store, shopping baskets over their arms. When Longarm came in they looked at him— he was not sure just exactly how to read the expressions on them. They were not hostile. Exactly. But they certainly were not welcoming either.

The woman behind the sales counter asked, "Are you here with a delivery, friend? I heard no wagon arrive."

Longarm swept his hat off. "No, ma'am. I'm, uh, I'm looking for the barber hereabouts."

Her lips thinned in a very small approximation of a smile. "I am sorry. We have no barber."

"None?" he blurted.

"No, we do not. Is there anything else?"

"Yes, ma'am. I'll be needing a place to stay tonight. Is there a hotel?"

She shook her head.

"A boardinghouse then?"

"No," she said. "None."

"Then d'you maybe know of somebody, some home-owner that'd take a lodger overnight? I'd be willing to pay."

"Sorry, no."

"Nobody?" he blurted.

The woman did not bother to respond.

Longarm sighed. No half measures this time either. He was open and blunt about it. "Ma'am," he said with all the patience he could muster, "is there a hardware?" He was thinking that maybe these women were feeling spooked from having a man in their midst. Perhaps he would do better trying to talk with one of the men of this town.

The woman smiled with evident relief. "Yes, friend, we do indeed have a hardware. It is in the next block," she pointed, "on the opposite side of the street. On the far corner, last store in that block. You can't miss it."

"Yes, ma'am, thank you. I have my horse tied at the loading dock out back of your place. Is it all right if I leave him there for a spell?"

"Yes, certainly."

"Thank you, ma'am. Thank you very much." Longarm

77

turned and strode outside, slapping the Stetson back on as he did so. Lordy!

The hardware was where she'd said it would be. Longarm entered and once more had to take his hat off. There was a woman behind the counter. The place, however, was an ordinary hardware mercantile. There were ready-made cut nails, bolts, bar iron, saws, files, hammers, all the usual stuff a body would expect to find in a hardware. It had that same, faintly metallic smell of all such stores.

"Ma'am, is the proprietor available?" Longarm asked of the stout, middle-aged woman behind the counter.

She smiled at him. "I am the proprietor, friend. What may I do for you?"

"But . . ." He shook his head. "Never mind. Could you direct me to the post office please, ma'am?" Surely Postmaster Lily would be able to help him figure this place out.

The hardware saleswoman was pleasant and friendly as she could be. "Certainly. It is in the next block down," she pointed back in the same direction he'd just come from. "On this side of the street. Next to last door on the block."

"Thank you, ma'am. Thank you very much."

Once again Longarm spun about and headed for the door. Harrisonville. Nice folks. Don't be too quick to judge. Huh!

Chapter 17

Longarm found the post office, all right. But there was no sign of the postmaster in it. Nor anyone else, for that matter. No postmaster, no clerk, no customers.

There was a thick coating of dust on the counter, and the bank of pigeonholes inside the cage was totally empty.

The door was unlocked, and anybody could have walked in and made off with . . . hell, maybe there wasn't anything there to steal.

Longarm went inside and entered the caged-off area that by law was reserved for authorized agents of the post office. Or, as in this case, authorized agents of the government of the United States of America. Which at this moment he figured he was.

A metal rack with spring-clips attached to it held a tidy assortment of rubber stamps. Below them was an ink pad. No ink had ever been poured onto the pad. Longarm took down one of the rubber stamps. Do Not Fold, that one would have said if used. But it never had been used. The reddish-brown rubber underside of the stamp was as virginal as the ink pad on the counter beneath it. Longarm returned the stamp to its place.

He pulled open a drawer situated immediately in front

of the dust-covered stool where a clerk would sit if there was a clerk present to do any sitting. It was a cash drawer with compartments built in toward the back of an exact size to hold currency sorted into several denominations and smaller compartments along the front where gold and silver coins might be placed.

Except there were no coins in the drawer. Nor currency. Nor even any dust in this case.

Postage stamps. In most postal cages the stamps were kept in a drawer handy to the clerk, generally beside the cash . . . ah! There. The stamp drawer had a barrel cylinder lock built into it. The lock was not locked. The drawer was open. Longarm pulled it partway out.

Harrisonville's post office had postage stamps available if anybody wanted to buy one. Folder upon folder of them. Hundreds of them. Maybe thousands. One cent, two cent, three and ten and twenty five and . . . hell, they had all manner of stamps.

Longarm leafed through several of the folders at random. Every sheet of stamps was whole, intact, complete with not so much as a ragged edge having been torn off. The supply of stamps was as complete as the day they were . . . no. No, that wasn't right, he realized when he came to the bottom-most folder. That one held a single sheet of stamps worth five dollars each. Those would carry parcels or really heavy envelopes. And from the sheet of fifty, four stamps had been removed.

Crazy. Just crazy as hell, Longarm figured.

But they were nice folks. Once you got to know them. So said Roger Billingsley.

Longarm thought about perching himself on the postal clerk's stool and waiting there to see just how long it would be before the man returned to his station.

Then, considering the dust and the paucity of activity here, he realized that might be a very long wait, indeed.

He checked to make sure he'd put everything back the way he'd found it, then went outside to make another stab at getting to know the nice people of Harrisonville, Wyoming Territory.

Chapter 18

"I'm looking for the postmaster, ma'am," Longarm said politely, hat in hand. "His name is Lily."

The woman smiled. "You mean Bonnie."

"No, ma'am, his name ain't Bonney. It's Lily. A Mr. Lily. That's who I was told to ask for."

The woman's smile turned into a friendly laugh. "Impossible," she said.

"Ma'am?"

"The post*mistress* is Bonnie Francine. I believe she does go by the last name Lily. Mine is Daffodil."

"I don't b'lieve I follow what you're sayin', ma'am."

"All of us have adopted new names for this new and wonderful place. We favor the names of flowers, although that is not mandatory. I suppose we could choose something else if we wanted. I don't think anyone has done so yet, but it could happen."

"Ma'am, I haven't the least idea what you're talkin' about here."

"The Society, sir. Are you not aware that . . . no, I see that you are not. Come inside out of the sun, please. The glare out here bothers my eyes."

"Yes'm." Longarm trailed the woman inside a shop,

into what proved to be a manufacturing facility in miniature where half a dozen women were assembling cunning little dolls and doll furnishings using corn husks, pieces of carved corn cob and other natural materials. The dolls were quite fetching, and no doubt would have been a delight to a little girl.

"Ladies," the woman Longarm spoke with on the street announced, "this gentleman is a visitor come to speak with our post*master*." She put some emphasis onto the *master* part of that word and drew a round of tittering from the workmen . . . workwomen . . . employees . . . in the place.

She turned back to Longarm. "Sir, this is Miss Hyacinth. Miss Chrysanthemum. Miss . . ." She went on around the room like that, pointing and smiling and telling off the names of a bunch of flowers. Then, she looked at Longarm again and smiled. "There is no Mr. Lily here, sir. As you can see, we are all ladies in Harrisonville."

"I don't understand," Longarm said. And that was the damned truth if ever he'd spoken it.

"We are a society of women who value the lives of all creatures," the woman explained. "We are also Druids."

Longarm was not entirely sure what a Druid was supposed to be. Except that he'd landed in the midst of some of them. Whatever they were.

"We worship the Goddess Moon and our Mother the Earth," Miss Daffodil went helpfully on. "And we are vegetarian."

Longarm scratched the side of his nose. "Reckon that leaves out any chance o' finding some pork chops for lunch."

Hell, he was only making some fun. From the reaction a body would've thought he dragged a skunk into the place and shot it in the butt right there in front of them. Two of the women gasped. A third got up and rushed out of the room with a hand clamped over her mouth as if she was about to puke up her toenails and was trying to get outside before she let fly. The rest of them all looked damn-all disapproving to say the least.

"Sir. Please! Don't say things like that."

"Sorry," Longarm mumbled. He wasn't. But it was what he was expected to say, and so he said it. Bunch of crazy damned bitches. "Look, d'you know where I can find this Bonnie Lily, the postmistress? I need t' speak with her, then maybe I can be on my way an' not cause you ladies any more discomfort."

"I shall take you to the Mother," Daffodil said.

"We're all of us already standin' on the earth," Longarm said with what he thought we impeccable logic.

"I do not mean Mother Earth. I refer to Mother Corn."

"Oh." He thought for a moment, then said, "But didn't you tell me . . . never mind." Corn has flowers, too, he supposed. Sort of. Not what you generally think of when it comes to flowers, but what the hell. This bunch of lunatics didn't have to make any sense. And didn't.

The woman led him outside and down the street, chattering all the while, pointing out this and that and saying who worked or lived in whatever place they were passing. Longarm paid no attention. He was already looking forward to finishing up his business here and getting back to Denver where there were robbers and politicians—same thing, really, except one wore a mask and the other a tie—and whores and drunks and draymen. In short, where the world made sense to him.

"Come inside, please," the woman told him as she reached an otherwise unexceptional building on the main street of Harrisonville. "Once inside, you will remove your hat and that," she made a disapproving face, "that firearm. It will be dark inside. Do not fear. Someone will take your arm and guide you. When you approach the Mother, you will kneel before her. Wait until she gives you leave to speak. Then you may make your plea."

"You say I'm s'pposed to shuck my gunbelt an' let myself be led around by somebody I can't see an' then *kneel* in front o' some woman inside there?"

"Exactly so, yes." The woman beamed, just as happy looking as if she had good sense.

"Lady," Longarm said, "that will be the fucking day."

He stepped around the woman who'd guided him here and opened the door wide. Thick curtains inside the vestibule kept any sunlight from reaching whatever lay beyond.

Well, piss on this, Longarm thought. He shoved the curtains brusquely aside, allowing a broad shaft of daylight to flood the place.

The room he saw in front of him looked like a child's fairy tale illustration for a queen's quarters, throne and all. The decor was red velvet and gold leaf, everything made to look like flowers and vines and leafy stuff.

A pair of young women wearing white robes flanked the entrance, and perched high on an ornate, gilded chair was a wizened old crone who looked like she should've died of a combination of old age and meanness twenty years ago.

There was a shriek of protest from the woman behind him, and two matching squeals from the acolytes at the doorway.

He could hear, but not see, a scurrying of bare feet in the farther shadows. Sounded to him kind of like rats running for their bolt-holes when a barn door is flung open unexpectedly.

The only light in the place until Longarm intruded came from a dish of oil with a tiny wick floating in it and an equally small flame rising from the wick, although in the light streaming in past the now open curtains, Longarm could see there were half a dozen torches set on cast-iron lamp stands, three on either side of the throne.

Before the acolytes could get their wits about them and

85

close the curtains behind him, Longarm used the lamp flame to touch off a match and used that to light the twin banks of torches.

The old biddy on the throne blinked in this harsh flood of brightness.

Longarm saw a picture in a magazine once of one of those Egyptians that'd been dead for a couple thousand years. Mummies, they called them.

This woman in front of him now looked kind of like a mummy, wrinkled and ancient and dry. Except this one was breathing.

It took her several moments for her eyes to adjust to the light. Then she looked him over closely. "You do know how to make an entrance, young man."

Chapter 19

Longarm grinned at her. "Why, thank you, ma'am. I do like t' bring light inta folks's lives."

The old bat was not without a sense of humor. She tipped her head back and brayed like a gut-shot burro. About halfway through this noise Longarm figured out that she was laughing.

"Daffodil, dear, you look like you are about to burst. Don't worry, sweetheart. It is perfectly all right. Our guest is not familiar with our ways, you see." Then her expression hardened, and she turned her attention back to Longarm. "I do want to point out to you that you are trespassing on private property. That could get you in trouble with the law."

"Yes, ma'am," Longarm said. "But if I may argue in my own defense, I didn't come here on my own. I was brought here. By one o' your folks, namely Miss Daffodil there."

"Do you think that defense would stand up in a court of law, young man?"

Longarm wasn't all that damned young. But, then, to this ancient crone, most any human person short of Methuselah would look young. "Yes'm," he told her, "I expect it would. 'Specially since I happen t' be the law here."

"Because you are a man and are carrying a firearm? Allow me to assure you, sir, that I write the laws in this town."

"Ma'am, it ain't . . ."

"Her name is Mother Corn," one of the acolytes hissed at him.

"Shame on you," another put in. That one, Longarm noticed, wasn't as butt ugly as most of this crowd was. At least this one looked like she was on the sunny side of forty. And her face hadn't been carved out of dried and cracking mud. Longarm winked at her, and she recoiled as if he'd slapped her instead.

Longarm turned his attention back to the elderly party on the throne. "Ma'am," he repeated with a sideways glance at the pissed-off acolytes, "it ain't my gun that gives me authority in your town. It's the badge that I'm carrying. I'm a deputy U.S. marshal, ma'am, and I come here on official business."

"I see. Very well. You may state your business."

"My business ain't with you, ma'am."

"All matters in this community are my business, young man."

"That's fine, ma'am. You do things your way; I'll do things mine. Between us we can maybe get this taken care of an' I'll be on my way."

"What is it that you want here, sir?"

"I need t' see B. F. Lily, who I understand is the postmistress here."

"Oh!" the old broad muttered. For some reason she looked to be disconcerted by that very simple request. "I . . . I don't think . . ."

"Mother Corn," one of the women in the shadows put in. "Don't you remember? Bonnie Lily is . . . away."

The woman blinked and heavily swallowed a few

times. She went into a brief coughing spasm, which Longarm suspected was only a delaying tactic so she could gain some time to think about what she would say next. "I think . . . come back tomorrow, Mr. Marshal. I will arrange for you to speak with Miss Lily then."

Longarm thought about pressing the point. But what the hell. This wasn't the sort of job that had any kind of time pressure on it. Not, that is, beyond his own desire to get the hell back to Denver and civilization, where a man could find himself a glass of whiskey and a card game if he wanted.

"Yes, ma'am. Tomorrow."

"And if you please, Mr. Marshal?"

"Yes'm?"

"Please refrain from making any more of these dramatic but very disruptive entries, will you?"

Longarm grinned at her again. "I'll mind my manners, ma'am."

"And so shall I. Now if you will excuse me, Mr. Long, I shall return my attention to what I was doing before your arrival."

"Yes, ma'am."

Longarm was already out the door—the heavy curtains quickly pulled closed behind him and, he was sure, the torches probably extinguished by then as well—before it occurred to him that when inside he had introduced himself only by title.

He had not given the old witch his name.

Yet she'd called his name when he was leaving.

Now who the hell would have told her that?

More to the point . . . why?

Chapter 20

Harrisonville, Wyoming Territory, did not offer visitors very much in the way of entertainment. There was not a single saloon, hotel, whorehouse or honky-tonk anywhere in sight. It was depressing, dammit. Here it was, halfway through the morning, with most of a day still stretching out before him, and Longarm couldn't find any place where he might buy a beer or sit in on a card game.

Beer and cards? Hell, he still hadn't seen another male human person since he rode out from the HH Connected after breakfast. Harrisonville really did seem to be inhabited only by women just like that Daffodil woman said. Certainly that was all he'd yet seen.

But then, dammit, a town couldn't manage without men to do the real work, he figured. There had to be some. Somewhere.

Probably, he reasoned, the men were out working in the fields. He supposed he could look one up and approach the fellow for advice about where to find a little diversion.

Longarm paused to trim and warm and then slowly light a cheroot, then walked to the far end of town and beyond, toward the checkerboard layout of small farm plots.

Whoever built the irrigation ditching did a damned fine job of it, he saw as he came closer to the cultivated plots. And he was fairly sure that all this work had *not* been done by any bunch of females. Especially a bunch of women working without horses or oxen to do the heavy work needed to make the many ditches and flow gates that he could see here.

Made by women using hand tools? No damned way. Not a project this extensive and this well laid out.

Whoever did it, there was ample water available now for whatever a man might want to raise. This far north, the growing season would be short, but the soil here in the basin seemed loose and fertile enough. Longarm guessed the shortage of warm nights would be about the only restriction on the crops that could be planted here.

Most of the farms, he saw as he got closer, were planted to some variety of corn. The plants were nicely established, most of them at this point coming about to the tops of Longarm's stovepipe cavalry boots. Given the season . . . he wasn't sure, but he thought it would be kind of up in the air about whether corn would make a crop here or not. It could come up a couple weeks short of filling out the ears. Some years it might make, he thought, but many it would not. It wouldn't be something a man could count on, either way.

On the other hand, judging by what he'd seen in that little handicraft shop back in town, it could be that the grain would be a secondary matter here. There was no livestock to feed, and there didn't seem to be so many people that they would have to worry about needing every last kernel of corn for eating purposes. If it was dried husks and clean cobs they wanted, so as to make dolls and things from them, the growing season wouldn't be short enough to make a difference. The cobs would be good for making dolls or tobacco pipes or any number of other things whether or not they filled out before harvest.

In addition to the corn, he saw beans, pumpkin, several varieties of squash, peppers, tomatoes—enough garden truck to fill a table. There would be no commercial market anywhere close by for the garden crops, so he supposed all of this was intended for use by the community members themselves. He was guessing that apart from the corn this was essentially one huge subsistence garden. It looked like the folks in Harrisonville intended to get along without importing much of anything outside their own community.

He paused to smoke and look around a bit and had to conclude that regardless of their future intentions, they'd brought an awful lot in when they were establishing the place. The lumber needed to build all this had to be bought elsewhere and hauled in along with the hardware—nails and hinges and glass and so on—in order to make these buildings. About the only community materials native to the site were the dirt and the water. Everything else came from a distant someplace. Including the people.

"May I help you?"

The voice that came from behind was soft and melodious. Longarm turned. While he'd been peering back at the town, this woman had come up behind him.

He smiled down at her. Quite a way down, for she was a very small woman. He suspected she would tape out several inches short of five feet, and standing next to him, she didn't seem much more than belt-buckle high. Wouldn't hardly have to crouch to reach his . . . ah, no. Not a good idea to think along those lines, he was sure. All she was doing was offering a friendly greeting to a stranger. Longarm snatched his Stetson off and held it in both hands. "Ma'am," he greeted.

The woman smiled at him. He couldn't get much of a look at her because she wore a wide-brimmed floppy hat that protected her face and neck from the sun. He could see that her cheeks were freckled and that her lips looked soft and full. But he couldn't see anything of her eyes and had no idea what color her hair was.

She wore bib overalls and a thin shirt buttoned high to the neck and was barefoot. The overalls effectively concealed her shape, apart from the fact that she was small of body in addition to being so short. She wasn't quite small enough to be considered a dwarf, he thought. But she wasn't real far from it, either.

"I asked if I could help you," she said. "Is there someone or something you are looking for?"

"No, ma'am . . . that is, well, yes, ma'am . . . I mean . . ."

She laughed, the sound pleasant and gentle.

"What I meant to say, ma'am, is that I was looking to talk to one of the menfolk of Harrisonville."

"You won't find any here, sir."

Longarm looked over her head—easy enough to do, as even with her hat on she didn't come any higher on him than his chest—toward the people chopping weeds and loosening soul out along the crop rows. A good half of them looked like men.

Then, he looked down at this helpful little woman and realized that from a distance she, too, would look like a man because of the utilitarian clothes she was wearing. "There aren't any men in the fields there?"

"Not a one," she told him. "We are all women here."

"*All?*" he asked.

She nodded. "Every one of us," she said cheerfully.

"You women built all this?" He gestured toward the irrigation ditching, then back toward the town buildings. "You ladies?"

The little woman shook her head. "No, of course not. We hired labor. Contracted the work out. That was all handled before our arrival."

"I see."

"Mother Corn wanted us free of worldly distraction, so all of this was complete before we came. There has scarcely been a man here since that day."

"Why?" Longarm asked.

"Oh, it isn't anything personal. I mean, we do not hate or despise you males. Nothing like that. We just find that we are more free to pursue enlightenment and truth when we are free of the demands and the emotional distractions that you—that men in general, I mean to say—bring with them."

"Enlightenment an' truth," Longarm repeated.

Her smile was one of gentle patience. "Exactly."

"An' have you found either o' those things?"

"The concept is not one of acquiring something and then being able to take it and leave," the woman said. "It is something one lives and celebrates after it has been found. And yes, thank you, I believe I have found both of those things and peace as well."

"In that case, ma'am, I'm happy for you."

"Thank you." The normally trite and meaningless words sounded perfectly sincere when this woman spoke them. She sounded genuinely grateful for the thoughts that lay behind his comment.

"Was there something you wanted to ask a man that I cannot help you with?" she asked, returning to the main point of her having come to greet him.

"Well, uh . . . is there someplace in town where a man . . . where a person, that is t' say . . . where a person can find something to, um, drink? Or something?"

The little woman's laughter was loud enough that heads were turning two fields away.

Chapter 21

It was bad enough to learn there was no place in Harrisonville where a man could buy himself a drink. What was really disconcerting was to discover there was nowhere in Harrisonville where a man could buy *anything*.

He guessed it just hadn't fully sunk in what that little farmer-woman was saying. Or something. It was one thing, though, to accept the idea that there wasn't any liquor here or beer or card games or much of anything else. But when he walked back to town and found a store that had coffee and salt and flour and suchlike on its shelves, he got an even bigger disappointment.

"Oh," the plump, gray-haired store clerk exclaimed when he said he'd like to buy some vittles, there not being anything in town that resembled a cafe or restaurant. "I don't know . . . you see, sir, we don't deal in," she hesitated for a moment as if the word she was about to say was something vulgar, "we do not deal in money, sir."

"Ma'am?"

"Money. You know."

"Yes, ma'am, I expect I know what that is all right. But what d'you mean you don't deal in it?"

"We are a community, sir. A family really. Would you

charge your sister for a mouthful of food if she came into your home to visit? Certainly not. Nor do we ask our sisters to pay for whatever they may need. We enjoy the products of our labors equally, each to her needs, each to her desires."

Longarm frowned. "What about this stuff?" He pointed toward a bag of salt, a barrel of wheat flour, a keg of molasses. None of those items were produced here. Each of them had to be bought and hauled in, and wherever they came from, the seller would surely have to have been paid in cash. So would the freighters.

The woman looked puzzled for a moment, then seemed to understand his question. She shrugged. "I would not know about that, sir. The Society provides for all our needs, whatever they may be. The merchandise, if you want to call it that, was already in place when I was asked to serve here. Beyond that, I really do not know." She paused, then brightened. "You could ask Mother Corn. The mother knows *every*thing," the chubby woman gushed.

Longarm got the idea that she quite literally meant that preposterous claim. She honestly believed that that Mother Corn person knew every-damn-thing.

"So how," Longarm asked, "would I go about getting something to eat around here?"

"Goodness gracious." She stopped, her brows knitting in concentration. "I do not believe we've ever had anything like this come up before. I really do not know, sir."

"I couldn't pay you for a few things an' then you turn that over to the . . . whoever they are?"

"Oh, no. Money is filthy, you know."

Longarm couldn't say that he'd known that before this moment, but he didn't interrupt her to say that.

"The very concept of money is degrading to the spirit, you see. Money is selfish and . . . and . . . ," he could tell she was trying to remember by rote the words she'd been

96

taught, but obviously did not fully comprehend, ". . . and money is . . . degrading. Did I mention degrading? And selfish. And . . . and . . . money is evil. A tool of the dark spirits." She looked relieved once she remembered that phrase about dark spirits. She smiled at him like she was pitying his male ignorance when it came to the subject of money, and what a terrible thing it really was.

"So I couldn't buy something to eat," he said.

"Oh, no. That would be very wrong."

"Then could you give me something so's I could make myself some dinner?"

The woman's brow furrowed again. This thinking stuff was not her precise cup of tea. "Oh, I . . . I don't know about that. You are not a member of the Society. And I've never . . . this has never come up before. I really should apply to ask the Mother about your question."

"You've never had visitors in the store before now?" Longarm asked.

She shook her head. "Never."

"No strangers here at all?"

"No, none."

Crazy, Longarm thought. These women were all crazy in their thick heads. And they were even more strange than they were crazy. The whole damned bunch of them.

"So what do you suggest I do about getting myself something to eat?"

"I really . . . I am sorry, sir. I really could not say about that. But I shall ask for enlightenment. I need to know in case this sort of thing ever happens again." She sounded like she doubted that possibility, but wanted to be prepared for it just in case.

Longarm thanked her—for exactly what he himself was not entirely certain—and left the store that didn't sell anything.

It was coming on toward lunchtime, dammit, and breakfast was a long way back.

That Mother Corn person said the postmistress wouldn't be available until tomorrow, and he couldn't get any answers until he talked with her. So he was going to have to stay overnight at the very least, and that meant he was going to need some food to put in his belly in the meantime. He certainly was not willing to go empty until some time tomorrow when B. F. Lily might finally show herself.

Grumbling under his breath more than a little, Longarm left the main street and headed around toward the back of the storefronts to reclaim his horse.

Chapter 22

"You're back awful soon, Marshal."

"Y'know," Longarm said, as he stood in the cookhouse doorway with his hat in hand, "I kinda get the idea you aren't surprised."

The scrawny cook named Chubby grinned at him. "Happens alla time. Bullwhackers and like that. They haul into that place the first time, they expect to make a regular delivery, relax a little, move along. The usual. You know?"

Longarm knew what the man was talking about. He'd expected exactly the same as the freighters apparently did.

"They end up coming here for their grub. Happens every time. Second trip if there is one, they come prepared. Make themselves a camp alongside one of the creeks. But the first time, they all end up here. Just like you done. Do you want I should cook you something, Marshal? The boss said you was to be treated right if you showed up again."

"If?" Longarm asked.

Chubby's grin flashed again. "That's the way he said it. I expect he knew good as I did that it was really 'when' and not 'if' but what he actually said was 'if'." The cook motioned for Longarm to come inside. "Steak be all right? Fried taters? Mayhap some greens to go with that?"

Longarm's mouth watered. It was the middle of the afternoon, and he hadn't had a bite to eat since before dawn. And that had been right here in this same cookhouse. "Forget the greens. Make up the difference with some extra fried potato."

"You got it, Marshal. Won't take me but a few minutes. Help y'self to some coffee while you're waiting."

It was a relief to be back to where there were other hairy-faced males in sight and horses and food and all that sort of thing. To be back, in other words, where things were normal. Longarm hung his Stetson on a peg near the door and made free with the HH Connected's coffeepot.

"Are you sure you don't want to carry a lunch with you, Marshal?" the foreman offered after breakfast the following morning. "It would be our pleasure to put something together for you."

"You've done more than enough already, Mr. Billingsley, putting me up two nights, feeding me all this time." He smiled. "Besides, I expect to be back here by lunchtime and have a hot meal 'stead of a bag lunch. My business in Harrisonville shouldn't take twenty minutes. I'll ride over there, do what I have to do and turn right around."

Billingsley nodded. "That's fine then. I'll tell Chubby to expect you. Not that the boys and I will be here. We have work to do. But we'll see you at suppertime."

"Thanks, but I don't expect to stay another night. I'll beg one of Chubby's fine meals again, then ride on east. I'm wanting to get back to Denver quick as I can." He extended a hand to the foreman. "Sure do want to thank you, though. And I hope you'll tell Mr. Harrison that I'm mighty grateful t' him, too, for all this hospitality. I hadn't

100

expected to need it or I could've packed some grub along." His smile grew bigger. "My own cooking wouldn't have been half as fine as what I've gotten here, of course, so I can't claim to be all that disappointed with the way things worked out." He hadn't seen Harrison this time. Billingsley mentioned something about the owner having gone down to Cheyenne on business, otherwise Longarm surely would have been invited to eat in the big house.

"Good luck to you, Marshal," Billingsley said as he shook Longarm's hand.

"And t' you."

The foreman went off to catch up with the HH Connected cowhands, most of whom were already saddled and mounted and waiting for the foreman to join them. Over by the corral, one of the green broncs decided to put on a show for the bunch and went into a frenzy of snorting from both ends and trying his level best to put his rider into the dust. The boy in the saddle hadn't noticed, but one of his pals had precipitated the pre-dawn rodeo by using the toe of his boot to goose the until-then quiet Cayuse. Longarm chuckled softly under his breath. Both the horses and the hands were rank and rested and eager at this hour.

Longarm had another cup of coffee, so the working folk could get done what needed doing and be off about their business without him getting in the way, then he went out to saddle his horse and head back to Harrisonville for that promised talk with Postmistress Lily.

He'd been a little later leaving the HH Connected this morning than he did yesterday, and the farm women were already in their fields by the time Longarm came in sight of the town.

It amused him to note that at least one of the Harrisonville residents looked to be interested in a diet consisting of more than just vegetable stuff, because down at the east end of town, the direction Longarm was riding in from, he could see one of them hunkered down beside the creek below the irrigation gates.

The figure was mostly obscured by a little brush that was growing up along the stream. Probably thought she was hidden, he suspected. So maybe that one did not want her 'sisters' to know she wanted some fish on the table. That surely was what she was doing there.

Longarm spotted her, but did not stare at her lest one of the others notice and wonder what he was looking at. He didn't want to give her away. Instead, he concentrated on looking toward the town.

Probably, he thought, his best bet would be to go back to that dark and gloomy chamber where Mother Corn held firm control over her flock. Or garden. Bunch of damned posies, maybe they considered themselves a garden instead of a flock.

The idea of coming up with a name for what a bunch of crazy damned Druid women would call themselves amused him. A bouquet, he thought? A bundle? Or, hell, simply a bunch.

He . . .

He heard a dull, moist sound like that of a slab of meat being whacked by a tenderizing hammer, and he felt the horse stagger.

Oh, shit!

He felt the horse's knees give way just about the time he heard the report of the rifle shot from off to his right—over at just about the point where he'd spotted what he thought was a fisherman in the weeds—and he slipped his boots out of his stirrups so he could jump clear as the horse fell.

He pushed off to his left, the side away from the rifleman—riflewoman in this case, he assumed—and was falling clear, reaching for the buttstock of his Winchester so he could drag the carbine out with him and be ready to go on the attack once he hit the ground.

The horse, damn it to hell anyway, twisted and whinnied loudly in pain. The unexpected movement contorted the animal's body, and, instead of falling to the right as Longarm expected, it went down to its left. It fell on the same side Longarm was on.

Longarm hit the ground hard, and, before he could roll aside, nine hundred pounds of dying cayuse came down on top of him.

The horse thrashed wildly for a moment, then went suddenly rigid and collapsed in dead—quite literally dead—weight directly on top of Longarm's legs.

"Son of a *bitch*!" he snarled as he tried to pull himself free.

From over toward the creek he heard a most unexpected sound. Not the report of another gunshot, but the hoofbeats of a racing horse.

Apparently the gunman had a horse hidden over there, too. Which probably meant—no, which almost certainly meant—that whoever shot at him was not one of the Druid women of Harrisonville.

The ladies might or might not be willing to act as the assassins of deputy U.S. marshals. Longarm would reserve judgment on that subject. But he was fairly sure that none of them had a horse to escape on.

But who the shooter could be—and why—those questions would have to wait until he could work himself out from under this dead horse. DammIt!

103

Chapter 23

"I don't think it is broken," the tall, hatchet-faced woman said as she felt his leg. "It is badly bruised, and I think both joints have been sprained. But no, I do not believe the bones broke. You were lucky."

Longarm didn't feel any kind of lucky. Well, no kind of luck other than bad, that is.

He hadn't been able to drag himself out from under the dead horse. The weight was just too much and his left leg was pointing in one direction while his boot and the foot inside it were turned back the other way, the whole painful mess held flat by the weight of the horse.

Fortunately, some of the women in the nearer fields saw what happened and came running, several of them still carrying the hoes they'd been using to weed the crop rows. Even with Longarm pushing and the women tugging, it hadn't been enough to lift the horse so Longarm could crawl out from under, but once they used the hoe handles to get some leverage on the deal, they took enough weight off that Longarm was able to get clear.

That hadn't been the end of it though. He stood up. And immediately fell down again.

He somehow kept himself from screaming like a son

of a bitch, but the pain was just damn near bad enough to make him pass out. As it was it made him bad sick to the stomach, and he thought he was going to puke.

It felt like both his knee and his ankle were busted to splinters. This Druid woman now—she was their healer and had been rushed out from town as quick as the farmer women knew she was needed—seemed to think that wasn't so, that there was nothing actually busted.

That was not a diagnosis Longarm hoped would be proven wrong. Sprains were bad enough. Two broken joints on one leg would be a real pain in the ass.

"Impatiens," the healer—Longarm hadn't caught her name—said to one of the young, rather sweaty farm women, "run fast as you can. Tell Mother Corn what has happened here. I need her wisdom, Impatiens. Hurry, please."

"Yes, Lady Aster." The farmer nodded her head and took off at a high lope for Harrisonville. She was one of the ones who chose to wear overalls to the fields. Bad as the pain still was, Longarm couldn't help noticing that Impatiens had a nice butt. Round and not too big.

He lay on the ground waiting, ringed close around by pretty near all the women who'd been working the farm plots. The little bitty one he'd spoken to the day before was there, he noticed. She was still wearing the bib overalls and floppy hat, but now that he was looking at her from below her level—not easily done with such a shorty, except now he was lying on the damn ground—he could see she had vibrantly blue eyes and curly blonde hair.

She was . . . *cute* was the word that came quickly to mind. Freckles. Small mouth. Button nose. Uh huh, cute.

The others were mostly a drab lot with short hair and plain features enlivened only by sweat and dirt.

The healer—Impatiens had called her Lady Aster—was on the wrong side of middle age, with a leathery complexion and steel gray hair braided into a no-nonsense rope that hung down her back to waist level. If the braid was that long, her hair would've extended well below her butt if it was let loose and combed out. Longarm liked long hair, even if it was gray. There was something about it that . . .

Several of the farm women gasped, and Lady Aster looked disapproving as idle thoughts and the presence of so many women gave Longarm a raging hard-on. The little blonde laughed. And did not turn her eyes away like the others did.

Lady Aster eliminated the source of embarrassment in a most effective if indirect manner, however. She reached down and quite unnecessarily gave Longarm's left ankle a squeeze.

His body stiffened at the renewed onslaught of sharp pain. And his previously stiff middle leg went instantly soft.

He glared at Lady Aster. She smiled a little and said, "No, I really do not think anything is broken."

"No," Longarm agreed in a dry, uncomplaining voice. "I reckon not."

Impatiens returned with a handcart and more Druid women. "Can he be moved?" she asked.

"Yes, of course."

"Mother Corn said you're to put him in your back room."

Lady Aster gaped, her jaw quite literally dropping open. "I can't . . . it may be days before he can walk again."

"Tell that to Mother Corn, not me," Impatiens said. Longarm got the impression the younger woman received no small amount of satisfaction from the healer's discomfort with the instruction.

Lady Aster mumbled something under her breath, then stood aside and motioned for the women with the handcart to pick Longarm up and lay him on it. She also waved for the farm women to go back to their fields.

It hurt like a wild bitch when the others moved him onto the unpadded cargo box of the handcart, and his leg was not well supported there. Worse, the cart bumped and bounced when they wheeled it back to town, and bolts of gut-wrenching pain drove through him with the least small jolt or jostle.

None of the women seemed to particularly give a shit about his discomfort, though.

Not that he was complaining. He'd have been a hell of a lot worse off if the asshole with the rifle had fired while he was still distant from Harrisonville. At least this way the women had seen and had come to help.

If he'd been out on the grass by himself and not able to free himself from the dead horse, it could have been bad. Mighty bad.

So he supposed he should count blessings here instead of bitching about how much he was hurting.

He supposed.

The cart bumped over some small obstruction on the ground, and Longarm bit his underlip to keep from crying out aloud at the pain.

Chapter 24

The Druid women were practically falling all over themselves with hospitality. In fact, he kind of hoped they would fall all over themselves. Some of them anyway.

The healer had been told to take him home and see to him. Well, she was seeing to him all right. She'd stuck him into a lean-to storeroom on the back of her place. There were no windows, no circulation of air and no furnishings except some shelves pegged onto the wall that was shared with the house.

They'd laid down a pallet of quilts and cotton batting, all of it covered over with a piece of tarpaulin that he supposed was there to keep him from soiling anything with his male presence.

He had no pillow, no blanket and so far nothing to eat. He wasn't sure what time it was, but he could no longer see bright daylight through the cracks around the door. There was still some pale light in evidence there, so he assumed it was evening or soon would be.

He was hungry. More than that, he was thirsty. Hunger is something a man can put up with if he's of a mind to. Ignore hunger pangs and in fifteen or twenty minutes they will go away. But thirst, now that is a different matter entirely. Thirst only grows worse with time, and all the more so if you think about it. And with nothing else to entertain him, Longarm thought about it. Constantly, except when he was mentally cussing and snarling at Lady Aster, the gray-haired old bitch.

Twice, he'd tried standing up and hobbling out in search of water and maybe some food. That had not been a good idea. Movement made his knee and ankle joints feel like some son of a bitch was holding a torch to them. And the thought of putting any weight on them? No, thank you. It was bad enough now to make him wonder if Lady Aster was wrong in her opinion that nothing was actually broken.

The last time he tried to stand was no more successful than the first had been, but while he was sitting more or less upright, he took the opportunity to reach down and feel his knee, which he could reach without too much trouble. He couldn't reach the ankle without bending the knee, and he damn sure wasn't up to that yet.

Still, after feeling it himself, he had to conclude that the old bitch of a healer was right. There wasn't anything broken. Just twisted way the hell farther than that joint was ever intended to turn. Another couple days maybe, then perhaps he could get around.

Of course, at that point he would have to decide if he should appeal to Mother Corn for permission to stay here—*with* something to eat and drink, that is—until a freight wagon came in or try to hoof it the eight or so miles out to the HH Connected.

The thought of walking eight miles was daunting right now, but in a few days, and maybe with a crutch or cane or something . . . point is, a man does what has to be done. Never mind what that may be. If it had to be done, he would find a way. Somehow.

For the time being though, about all he could hope to do was lie here in his own sweat and wait for someone to come offer him a bite to eat and something to drink.

If he was lucky.

Chapter 25

"I brought you some supper." The words were pure music. By the time he felt some air indicating the door had been opened, it was full night. No night is ever completely dark, of course, so he could see the outline of someone silhouetted in the open doorway, but could not see who that person was.

"Come on in, then. Thanks." He let the hammer gently down on the big Colt he'd grabbed as soon as that door opened. Not being able to see who was there except for a black-on-charcoal outline hadn't given him any reason to feel his guest couldn't be that rifleman coming in to take another shot at him.

The person at the door stopped. "Was that . . . did I hear a gun being cocked?"

"No, ma'am, just the opposite. An' don't fret. I only shoot people on purpose. I couldn't possibly shoot you till after you've given me that food you're carrying."

The voice chuckled a little and came forward. She was much less visible as she moved away from the thin moonlight near the doorway. "Damn," she blurted as Longarm heard the sound of something light being kicked and skittering out of the way.

Longarm felt the side of his pallet sag just a little as she felt her way to a seat beside him, the fingers of her free hand brushing lightly against his hip. "I dunno what you have there, but it smells mighty fine," he said.

"It's cornbread," she said, "hot from the oven. We don't have any butter, but I drizzled some honey on it."

He grinned, forgetting that she would not be able to see. "Shucks, I was hoping for a steak and some taters fried in hog lard."

"You were not. Now, do you want these corn dodgers or don't you?"

"You know I do," he said. With more than a little effort, he raised himself into a sitting position and dragged himself backward on the pallet until he was leaning against the wall, using that as a backrest. The girl—he had no idea who she was—found his hand and pressed the crumpled neck of a cloth sack into it. The size and texture suggested it was a flour sack.

The corn dodgers inside were as she'd said, still warm and fresh, and when he opened the mouth of the bag, their aroma filled the small shed. Longarm's mouth began to water so fast he had to swallow hard in order to keep from drowning himself in his own spit.

"Lordy, these are good," he said. It was true. "Did you bake them?"

"Oh, no. Each of us specializes. We have ladies who do nothing but bake."

"Well, you can tell them from me that they're mighty good at it." He took another mouthful of the moist, honey-sweet corn dodger, popped the rest of that one into his mouth and reached into the bag for another. "I don't s'pose you brought along anything to drink, did you?"

"No. Are you thirsty?"

"Huh. I haven't had anything t' drink since my morning coffee. I reckon it's fair to say that I'm thirsty."

"I'll go get you something. Wait here." There was a

moment of silence, and then he heard soft laughter.

"Yeah," he said dryly. "Reckon I will."

The girl stood, and, a moment later, he saw her silhouette again on her way outside. She wore a bonnet, a tight fitted bodice and wide, swirling skirts, but apart from that, he could tell nothing about who or what she was.

An angel, he supposed, that's what she was. And so was whoever baked these corn dodgers. He helped himself to another.

His benefactress returned in five minutes or so carrying a metal pail with a spout. He recognized what the thing was. It was one of those steel bucket contraptions intended for watering small plants. Not that he minded. He wouldn't care if the vessel she brought was a bull's nut sack if the thing held water.

She returned to the pallet, and once again sat beside him, guiding the heavy pail into his hands and retrieving the now empty flour sack from his lap. Her fingers brushed over the cloth at his fly. Longarm couldn't help but react to that. But he scolded himself for doing so, dammit. It was accidental because of the darkness, he was sure of that, for there was no hint of salaciousness in the woman's voice or manner here.

The pail was indeed one of those plant watering things. He had to screw the perforated end off it so he could drink from the spout. Of course he knew good and well he was only creating a different problem for himself when he did that. Take water in now, and he would have to let water out later. By morning he'd be needing to piss something awful.

But that was then. This was now. And he was almighty thirsty right now.

"Ahhh! That's better," he said. He set the pail down beside his pallet where he'd be able to reach it when he wanted another drink.

"All done?" she asked.

"Yes. An' I feel an awful lot better now, thanks."

"Would you be willing to do something for me, now?"

"Long as it doesn't involve jumping up an' running a foot race, yeah. I'd be glad to."

He heard a muted, furry sound that after a moment he recognized as a throaty chuckle. "Good."

And, a moment after that, he felt her hand on his fly again. Except this time it was no accident, nor any mistaking the favor she was requesting.

Chapter 26

Deft fingers unfastened the buttons at his fly and undid the buckles of both his pants and the Colt. Longarm doubted she noticed, but he did not allow the .44 to go along for the ride when she tugged the gunbelt free and laid it aside.

By the time she was done with all of that, he had a raging hard-on. Probably could've drilled holes in an adobe wall if he'd needed to.

"Oh, my. This morning I saw that it was big. But . . . oh, my."

He still didn't know which one she was, but she'd been among the bunch of flowers who'd helped him earlier. However reluctantly, they'd helped him, that was true. But he did not remember, until this woman mentioned it, that he'd lifted the front of his trousers with a woody. He gathered that this was not one of the Harrisonville women who'd acted offended by that.

She took Longarm's pecker out and very gently played with it, running her fingers over it, examining it by touch to the point that he doubted there was any part of his cock bigger than a fly speck that she hadn't stroked and massaged. Not that he was complaining.

"Can you raise your hips up just a little?" she asked.

"Yeah, I think so." Using his arms and right leg only, he levered his butt off the pallet.

"That's better." He felt her hands grab hold of his waistband at either side and pull, dragging his pants down so he was naked from his waist to a point just above his knees.

Her hand returned to his cock, then took a moment to feel his belly and thighs. "You're hairy."

Longarm said nothing. Hell, it was simple fact. No point denying it nor affirming what she already knew. Besides, she certainly didn't sound like she minded it.

She resumed touching him. That went on for some minutes—he was not complaining, but he *was* starting to ache a little from the overlong continued state of arousal— before she shifted position on the side of the pallet and bent over him.

Longarm felt her breast press soft against his thigh, the warmth of her flesh reaching him even through the layers of cloth that quite decorously covered her chest. She had made no move to disrobe.

The fingers of one hand remained in a loose circle around the base of his bumping, throbbing cock while her other hand gently cupped his balls. He felt a fingernail scrape lightly across that exquisitely sensitive flat that lies between the scrotum and the asshole. This girl was . . .

He damn near cried out aloud when he felt the head of his prick engulfed in moist heat. Half a moment later he felt a barely perceptible nip of sharp teeth on his shaft just below the head. Her use of teeth was deliberate, though, and intended to tease rather than hurt.

It worked. Not that he needed any further teasing. But it damn sure worked.

He felt her lips tighten below the bulbous head of his engorged pecker, and she began to suck.

Longarm cupped the back of her head in the palm of

his hand and sat there enjoying the bobbing of her head and the pull of wet suction on his cock. He was more than ready though and after only a few moments warned her, "If you don't stop that, you're pretty soon gonna have a mouthful."

She stopped and lifted her head barely far enough to allow his cock to slide free of her lips. "Can you make it a second time if you come now?"

"Yeah, of course."

"Good." She sounded pleased. "I'm thirsty, too. But not for water."

Once again he felt her lips engulf him, and this time she was serious in her intent. She took him deep, driving herself down onto his erection so hard he could feel it push far into her throat and past that tight ring of cartilage that guards the opening of the windpipe.

For one brief instant, he gave thought to the problems that would arise if she drowned herself in his come.

But that concern flickered into his mind and was almost immediately driven out again by the rising pressure of release that her sucking brought to him.

He felt the buildup of heat in his loins and the ripping explosive force of release as a fountain of semen erupted from his nuts and shot into her mouth.

Longarm groaned and squeezed her head so hard it must surely have hurt her, but if so, she did not complain about it. Instead, she pushed herself onto him all the harder and sucked him all the more vigorously, drawing out every last drop of come. He could feel her throat contract as she swallowed time and time again in an effort to keep up with the quantity of juice flowing hot and fresh from his gonads.

She sucked until surely there could not have been anything more for her to pull out of him, then finally sat up again. Her voice was cheerful when she said, "My good-

116

ness, but there was a lot of it, wasn't there? And tasty, too. Thanks."

He laughed. "You're welcome. Come back any time."

"Oh, I intend to. You did promise me seconds, if you recall."

"I didn't forget," he said.

"Good. Because neither did I." She stood up and did something, he couldn't see what, but heard the rustle of cloth. Then she dropped to the pallet beside him once more.

Her hand and then her mouth again found his pecker but this time only long enough to once again arouse him to a full and still powerful erection.

"Nice," she murmured.

"Mmm."

The girl pulled away from him, stood and straddled him with one foot placed on either side of his waist.

She fluffed her skirts wide and squatted, guiding his cock with one hand while she lowered herself onto him.

He felt the wet, eager lips of her pussy receive him, and she let her weight down onto him.

The jostling hurt his knee some. But not so much that he wanted her to move aside.

"Lovely," she whispered. "Lovely." She pressed herself downward, giving Longarm all her weight and taking all of his length inside her body. Then, she leaned forward, her hands on his shoulders, and probed his mouth with her tongue while she rotated her hips in the age-old grind and thrust known to every woman probably since birth.

"Lovely," she whispered once again and then trembled, her body growing stiff and shuddering as throes of pleasure washed through her.

Longarm smiled. And pulled her close for a kiss. She'd come, too. Now they were both even, the way he saw it, and could get on with the rest of things.

Which he intended doing right about now.

Chapter 27

Come morning, his knee was swollen to the size of a throw pillow and still hurt like a son of a bitch but the ankle was not nearly as painful as it had been to begin with. Any improvement was welcome, but this improvement was not yet enough to enable him to get up and walk. He knew that for certain sure, because he tried—twice—before accepting defeat.

And he'd been damn sure right about having to take a piss. His bladder was so full he began to get seriously worried that he might hurt something in his gut if he didn't find some relief. Unable to go look for a shitter, and having no desire to piss his pants, he made do by rolling to the edge of the pallet and letting go against the shed wall. There was a dirt floor so the urine would soak in. Eventually. And if he soiled their precious quilts, well, fuck 'em. If they wanted a good guest, they might first consider being good hosts.

Once he'd relieved himself he felt damn near human again. He lay back and waited, and a few minutes later—just as well it hadn't been a few minutes sooner—the shed door swung open and one of the flower women came inside.

Longarm looked at her, initially curious if this might have been his still unknown visitor from the night before.

It was not.

He was sure of that because this woman was a mound of suet piled almost as high as the door frame. And she'd gotten that way, Longarm marveled, without so much as a mouthful of bacon or gravy or fried chicken or any of the rest of those wonderfully fat and tasty dishes. Just vegetables. It seemed scarcely possible.

"Good morning," he said as she came in. "Have you been a member of the community very long?"

She eyed him suspiciously and said, "This town has not been here very long. None of us could be old residents."

"I meant have you been part of Mother Corn's order for long?" he corrected himself.

"No, only a few months."

"Ah," he said in what he hoped was a sage and kindly voice. "A novice. Good for you." What he was actually thinking was that this explained her bulk. She had fat left over from before she signed on as a Druid and had to give up meat as part of the agreement.

"I brought you something to eat," she volunteered. She was carrying a small pail or growler of the sort used in more civilized communities for the carrying of beer. It was covered with a small cloth, and, if there was a scent, he could not detect it even though Longarm's sense of smell was pretty good.

"Thank you." She handed him the pail, then turned and left without responding to his gratitude.

Not that he was complaining. She could've spit into the bucket first.

Come to think of it, maybe she did. Before she came inside the lean-to.

And what the hell. It was okay for her to leave now. He hadn't wanted a blow job from the fat, ugly broad anyhow.

119

He pulled the cloth back and peered inside. Hominy. He liked hominy well enough. Liked it cooked with salt and plenty of bacon. No bacon in this batch, he could be sure of that.

No one had thought to pack a spoon in the bucket, so he settled for dipping in with his curved fingertips and gobbling the soft hominy pellets off of them. The good news was that there was no danger of burning himself, the bad was that the hominy was cold. Probably left over from yesterday some time.

He grunted. He hadn't expected bacon, but there was no salt either.

Yeah, these women were mighty accommodating to visitors.

Well, that one last night had been. Longarm found himself smiling at the thought of her. Sure did wish he knew what she looked like though.

He settled in to the task of surrounding every last morsel of the cold and nearly tasteless hominy. A boy didn't want to let his strength run down, now did he?

The fat broad came back an hour, hour and a half later. Longarm could have kept track of the time by as simple a process as looking at his watch. But he didn't much give a crap, all things considered. He just lay there. Thinking. Not all of his thoughts were pleasant ones.

"Here," she said brusquely. She was carrying a length of one by four lumber that probably was left over from when the workmen built the houses here. It had been planed to size and not smoothed, but it seemed sturdy enough. He could not tell how long it was. A little more than five feet would have been his guess.

"Thanks, I'm sure, but I already picked my teeth."

"Don't bother trying to be funny. You are not welcome here. And you cannot make me like you."

"What a surprise," he drawled.

120

"Get up," she ordered.

"I can't." That was a lie. He was pretty sure that he could manage to get to his feet if he really wanted to. At the moment, and under this bitch's direction, he saw no compelling reason to be agreeable.

The fat woman did not argue. She bent down and picked him up.

Surprised? More than just a little. Obviously not quite all of that bulk was fat. There was some serious muscle in there, too.

She picked him up, set him onto his feet and shoved the board into his armpit like a crutch. It was several inches too short for comfort but all in all not that bad a fit.

The fat woman was on the short side, too. A little shorter than the board actually. From the way she'd filled the door frame coming and going, Longarm had assumed she was tall as well as being wide, but that was not so. It was just a very low doorway as he found out when he tried to limp outside with the assistance of the impromptu crutch. He had to duck low, and, even so, damn near gave himself a whack on the noggin.

"Where are my things?" he asked. His hat, saddle and Winchester failed to join him in the lean-to. He hoped no one stole them while he was on his back.

The woman did not answer. She merely pointed. Longarm recognized the building where Mother Corn held her dark and mysterious court.

He set out at a slow and deliberate pace. In the opposite direction.

Chapter 28

Well, that was good news. Enough to start a trend? He hoped so. In any event, omens and portents notwithstanding, his things were still lying there in the grass along with the dead and bloating horse. Charlie Boyd's horse, come to think of it. But he would deal with that later. Right now . . .

He felt considerably better once he had the hat on again. He was unaccustomed to being outdoors without it, and the combination of moving air and bright sunshine were disconcerting.

The rifle lay on the ground where he'd dropped it.

And the saddle, unfortunately, was still firmly strapped around the chest of a very heavy carcass. Longarm had good reason to remember how heavy the horse was. But he wasn't going to leave the saddle there another night for the field mice to chew on or for some passing soul to help himself to it.

He unfastened the girth, but even with the board for a crutch, he was not able to bend down and tug the saddle free of the dead weight. He tried several times before giving it up as a bad deal.

If he could get himself seated on the ground close to

the horse's back, he thought, maybe he could brace his good leg against the animal's butt and pull with both hands. That might be enough to drag the saddle loose. Or . . .

"Do you need some help?" a voice asked from behind him.

Longarm's head snapped around, and his right hand flashed to the butt of the big Colt. "Oh, I . . . sorry." He smiled. "There's not many folks can sneak up on me like that. This is twice you've done it. You move mighty light."

The little farm woman laughed. "That is a talent I never suspected having. It seems a shame it has no practical value."

"Oh, I dunno. You'd make a fine burglar. If you decide that peace an' enlightenment aren't exciting enough, that is."

Her laughter was even louder this time. "They are enough." Then she gave him an impish grin and added, "So far. And if I may repeat my question, what can I do to help you?"

"I'm tryin' to get my saddle loose an' can't quite manage it with this bum leg."

"How can I help?"

"I think if I use this here board to pry with I can lift the horse an inch or so. Then while I'm doing that if you could take hold of the pommel there and kinda drag it free I'd sure be obliged." A saddle horn would have been handy in a situation like this, but, of course, the military style McClellan did not have a horn.

"Let's try it."

The one-by crutch was too light to work as a pry bar. All it did was bend and threaten to break. And that would have left him with no support at a time when he really was not up to walking unaided.

"Wait a second. Let me try this instead." Longarm got

123

a firm grip in the horse's mane, braced himself and pushed with his right leg with all his strength. He could not lift the carcass off the ground, of course, but did take a considerable amount of weight off the cinches. The girl grunted and strained and, after a moment, dragged the saddle free.

"Wonderful, thanks. Are you all right? You're all red in the face. Which if you don't mind me sayin' so makes you look even prettier than usual."

The compliment made her blush. But he could tell that she liked it.

"Well do you?" he demanded.

"Do I what?"

"D'you mind me sayin' such a thing?"

She hesitated. Then shook her head. "I don't mind." That came out in a very small whisper.

"I appreciate your help, miss."

She peered up at him, acted like she wanted to say something, but changed her mind about whatever it would have been. Instead, she spun around and bent over the horse's head to strip Longarm's bridle from it and hand it to him.

Longarm shoved the Winchester into the boot that was strapped to the saddle, folded the bridle and tied it onto one of the cargo rings and wrapped everything into a tidy bundle using the stirrup leathers to secure everything together.

"Would you like me to carry that for you?"

It was beginning to occur to him that this small woman most likely was his visitor from last night. He hadn't seen the woman's face, but after discovering this morning how small that doorway opening was—and remembering back to how tall his nighttime visitor had been—yeah, it seemed very likely that this was the lusty little thing who'd been so pleasantly accommodating last night.

Longarm winked at her. "We could maybe go back to

124

town by way of the brush by the creek over there."

"What do you mean?"

"You know. Have a little privacy an' get sunburn in places that don't see the sun real often."

The little woman drew herself to full height.

And slapped the bejabbers out of Deputy U.S. Marshal Custis Long.

She had a pretty good right hand, and, for a minute or so there, he wasn't aware of his leg hurting at all.

Chapter 29

There was a bunch of high-pitched squealing and severe consternation when Longarm walked into the outer chamber at Mother Corn's abode. Sounded kinda like a bushel of rats dumped into a dog-fighting pit, he thought. Women in white robes disappeared with magical speed.

Longarm set his saddle beside the door and limped to the curtain-shrouded entry only to be met there by one of the white-robes. And not a bad looking one, except for probably being on the wrong side of forty. She would've been a real looker when she was in her prime. Wasn't too awful bad right now.

"Don't," she cautioned him before he could sweep the curtains open. "Please wait while we light the lamps. Mother Corn realizes that you are . . . uncomfortable . . . in the presence of the shadow spirits."

Longarm grunted. And waited. The old harridan was making a gesture of conciliation. Fine. He could do the same and not bust in on her again.

The acolyte disappeared inside the throne room—or whatever the hell they called it—and was back moments later. "Mother Corn will receive you now."

"Not so grand an entrance this time," the old bat said, peering at his crutch.

"Yeah, well, things happen. Y'know?"

"I have been informed of your misfortune."

"Misfortune, hell. I seen one of your people jump on a horse and hightail it after I was shot at."

"Whoever fired that shot, Marshal, it was most assuredly not one of my ladies."

"I couldn't get a good look at her, but it was a woman," he declared. "Had to be one of yours."

He was, of course, stretching the truth to unrecognizable proportions. He'd thought at the time that it was a woman he saw on the creek bank. But then, at the time, it was a woman he *expected* to see there. It could as easily have been a man wearing a duster to hide his regular clothing. At a distance, a pale duster could look very much like a dress. And Longarm had not actually seen the rifleman—riflewoman, whatever—make his or her escape. Longarm had been pinned underneath a dying horse at the time and was on the wrong side of it to be able to see who it was who'd shot at him.

But Mother Corn didn't need to know all the particulars. Longarm figured if he could put her on the defensive, maybe he could use that leverage to get a little cooperation around here. So far the cooperation he got was very little indeed.

"You are in error, Marshal. I can assure you it was no member of our colony."

"Yeah, well, we'll leave that question open for the moment. Now what was it you wanted to see me about?"

The old biddy blinked. "I?"

"The fat broad said you wanted t' see me," Longarm said. He heard a gasp of outrage from off in the shadows. Apparently the fat broad was lurking somewhere in that direction.

"Ah! Yes. I did ask that you be brought before me."

127

Brought before her indeed. The decrepit old bitch certainly liked to give herself airs, didn't she? Longarm was not in the mood to kowtow to any self-styled high priestess. Or whatever the fuck she thought she was. He thought it was time to show the respect he had for her and her summonses. He pulled a cheroot out of his coat pocket—a bent and slightly rumpled one, but still intact—bit off the twist and spit that onto the floor, then crutched his way over to one of the lamp stands and used the flame there to light his cigar. Mother Corn looked like she'd just swallowed a turd, and the other women in the room hissed like a room full of snakes.

Longarm looked at the old bag and said, "I'm here. An' I believe you said you'd have the postperson Lily here for me t' talk to."

"I did not summon you for . . ."

"Lady, I'm here on official U.S. gummint business. I don't have either the time or the inclination to piss around with you an' your fantasies. Just produce B. F. Lily. Her and me will have our talk. Then I'll go back where I came from an' not bother none of you no more."

"I am in charge here, young man. Not you."

"Bullshit." He blew a stream of pale smoke in her direction, and she made a sour face when the scent of it reached her. At least he thought that's what she was doing when her face wrinkled up like that. She was so naturally sour looking that it was a little hard to tell.

"Our dear Lily is not available to speak with you today."

"Why? She on the run after taking a shot at me, is she? Is that it? Is Lily the one that shot my horse?"

"Of course not. She . . ."

"Then drag her out here. Let me get a look at her. Like I said, I need t' see an' talk with her so's I can get on about my business and leave you crazy witches t' do whatever it is you do here."

128

"We are *not* witches," Mother Corn snapped as if he'd been serious when he used the term. "We are Druid. We worship the Earth, the Moon and the Stars. And *all* of our spells and spirits are benign. If we were witches, which we are not, we would be white witches. Not that I expect an ignoramus like you to understand the distinction."

Jeez, Longarm thought. After a comeback like that he had to figure that these women really did consider themselves to be witches. Sort of.

He'd thought they weren't screwed together very tight to begin with. Now he damn well knew it. They were fruity as Christmas cakes every one of them, and this Mother Corn harpy was the worst among them.

"Lady, do yourself and this bunch of lunatics a big favor. Fetch Lily out an' let me get shut of here. We'll all be a sight happier once I'm gone."

He didn't wait for her to answer, just turned around and stumped his way out, the effect no doubt somewhat diminished by the ill-fitting crutch but, hell, it was the best he could do under the circumstances.

He sure did wonder, though, what the big fucking deal was. All he wanted to do was have a few words with this postmistress and then go file a report on it. What was so complicated about that?

Chapter 30

Along about dark, he decided there were going to be no guest-type comforts tonight. No supper. And no pussy, either. Apparently Mother Corn's response to his request—okay, demand—to talk with Lily was going to be to ignore him. Probably in the hope that he would go away.

Not likely. Not even if he did have a way to leave. Which he did not. Not short of trying to walk eight miles on a bum leg with a slab of board for a crutch. Oh hell, he could do it if he really had to, he supposed. The good thing was that he did not really have to.

He did, however, intend to do a small amount of walking. He was hungry, he was thirsty and he was fairly thoroughly pissed off with this entire situation. The best thing to do, he decided, would be to fuck these women—figuratively speaking, that is; most of them seemed way too ugly for any sane male to do it in the flesh—and make do without them.

With that in mind, Longarm picked up his crutch and his saddle and hobbled out into the gathering darkness.

Thinking he was heading to a civilized place, he hadn't brought any food with him, but he'd packed plenty in the way of an appetite. That, however, was something he could satisfy without the assistance of the old witch. No, she objected to that term, better to think of her as the old bitch instead, he supposed.

He made his way past the glowing windows of Harrisonville's houses. The ladies seemed to be mostly in their homes having their meatless suppers. Very few of the "business" places—if that is what you called commerce where no money changed hands and profits were not sought—showed any lights.

Longarm wasn't even tempted to break into one of the stores where food could be obtained. Mother Corn probably would like nothing better than to file some sort of pick-nit complaint against him. If it would be only himself involved, Longarm wouldn't give much of a shit, but something like that could come down on Billy Vail, too—all the more so since Longarm's services were kind of on loan to the post office at the moment. Better not to take on that kind of grief.

He made his way through a couple alleys. Did take a look inside the post office building while he was at it in the hope he might find the elusive B. F. Lily there. No such luck. There was a lamp burning there, but the place was deserted. Again.

Not deserted still, however. Someone had definitely been there since Longarm's first visit to the Harrisonville post office. There was a pile of printed forms on the counter now next to the rack of rubber stamps and a matching pile of brown manila envelopes.

Civic affairs stuff, he saw when he glanced at the papers. Voter enrollment forms for the Crawford County rolls. Which figured. A busybody like Mother Corn would demand to have her say in whatever happened. And she would make damn certain every one of her tame flock voted precisely the way she told them to. Longarm hadn't a moment's doubt about that.

Not that he cared about any of that, however. What he

wanted here was the postmistress, nothing and nobody else. And Miz Lily wasn't to be found.

He made his way back out into the night and on toward the unimproved lower end of the creek, below where the irrigation ditching had disturbed the natural patterns of growth.

Between the creek and the underbrush along it, Longarm figured he could find all the supper he cared for. As good as a grocery store any old time.

Aside from the likelihood of finding fish in the creek, there should be small game aplenty in the thick brush. There probably has never been a truck garden planted that didn't attract rabbits and woodchucks and such. And of course the predatory birds that prey on small critters, too. So where would the rabbits go to hide from the hawks and the owls? Into the creekside brush, of course.

Longarm calculated that with very little effort, and only a small investment of time, he should be able to put together a decent meal.

Meat included, thank you.

And, what the hell, why not some leafy green stuff to go along with rabbit broiled over an open fire. He was sure he could filch a few items from the Druid farm plots. Carrots and shell peas and potatoes and like that. Turnips only as a last resort, though. Lordy, but he did despise turnips. He might well decide to stay hungry rather than eat a turnip. He made a sour face just from thinking about that.

He also made it to the creek before too awfully long and spent a few minutes deciding on what he wanted to do and where he wanted to do it.

Then, he set about the business of setting some snares and cutting willow withes to use for a fish trap. Not so sporting a method for catching fish but hell for effective.

He whistled half under his breath while he went about it.

132

Chapter 31

Longarm smiled at the faint sound of twigs cracking. Something in one of his snares, he concluded. And that made it sound like supper. The thought of rabbit roasted over an open fire was mouthwatering, indeed. He could as good as taste it. He . . .

He frowned, that smile replaced as the slight noises not only continued, they came nearer.

And now, closer, he could hear that this was not the sound of something thrashing in the grip of a snare, but the heavier crunch of feet moving through the brush.

Longarm cocked his head and listened closely. Footsteps, all right. Shuffling. Not human. A cow, perhaps? Or an elk this far from the safety of the high country?

Not apt to be an elk down here, and the HH Connected cowboys did a good job of keeping Henry Harrison's bovines well clear of Harrisonville. Maybe the sight of meat on the hoof offended the Druid women or something, but so far Longarm hadn't seen any cattle in the vicinity.

Not elk then. Not a cow. And definitely something much too heavy for a deer or pronghorn antelope.

Which by process of elimination kind of left . . .

Longarm hunched lower and waited as the footsteps

came closer and closer. The animal passed about a rod downstream from where he'd made his camp. It stepped out of the willows and splashed through the creek. Once outside the protective cover of the brush, there was starlight enough for him to clearly make out the animal. And the rider on its back.

The rider wore a white linen duster that showed up in the night like it'd been lighted. He also wore a wide-brimmed hat and carried something long and slim balanced across the pommel of his saddle. It didn't take much imagination to figure out what that object would be.

Looked like the man with the rifle was coming back to correct the oversight he'd made earlier when he shot at Longarm and hit the horse instead of the man.

The one small fly in his ointment was that Longarm was no longer lying asleep in that shed but sitting out here in the bushes waiting for quarry to come along. He just hadn't known what sort of hunting he would be doing.

The horseman rode slowly and quietly toward the mostly dark buildings of Harrisonville a few hundred yards distant.

Longarm followed, just as quiet, using the butt of his Winchester as a cane and gritting his teeth at the pain.

But then, the pain of a wrenched ankle wasn't spit compared with what a rifle bullet could do.

It was no fun at all, though, and both his knee and ankle felt worse and worse the further they went. There was no help for that, though. Longarm didn't think of this as being an optional outing. If this mounted intruder was indeed the same one who'd tried once already to kill him, Longarm wanted to know it for certain sure. And then do something about it.

He stayed low as he could and silent as man and horse entered the side streets of Harrisonville.

The man seemed to know exactly where he was going.

And Longarm had a damned good idea of the destination himself.

The guy didn't fuck around about it. He dismounted a block away from the shed where Longarm was supposed to be and went on foot from there. Straight to the shed door, not for a moment suspecting that anyone else was aware of his presence.

Not having any uncertainty about where he was going, either. He knew exactly which building he wanted. And what he was expecting to find there.

If he'd been really good at assassination, Longarm thought, he should have paid some attention to his own back trail just in case. But he did not. He crept straight ahead to the shed where Longarm was supposed to be sleeping and brought his rifle to his shoulder.

Silently, the SOB eased the shed door open just an inch or two and poked the rifle muzzle inside.

It would be dark in there, Longarm knew. The women hadn't left any lamp or candle for his comfort. Now that inconsiderate oversight worked to his advantage as the man with the rifle aimed down at the pallet where a pile of quilts substituted for the sleeping body of Custis Long.

All he likely could make out in the darkness was the barely visible shape of the pallet.

He stuck the barrel of the rifle in and hesitated not at all.

A flash of yellow flame momentarily lit up the interior of the shed and much of the surrounding alley. The sound of the gunshot seemed unnaturally loud in the night.

Longarm blinked, trying to regain night vision that had been destroyed by the muzzle flash.

He heard the metallic clatter of a rifle lever being jacked to seat another cartridge, and the gunman fired again. Then a third time.

Son of a bitch hadn't yet figured out that the place was

empty, Longarm thought with considerable satisfaction.

That was better than merely fine. While the man was busy congratulating himself for defeating a sleeping foe, Longarm could sidle up behind him and whack him one on the noggin. Put him in manacles and then get some answers, dammit, about why he was sneaking around trying to kill a deputy marshal whose only desire here was to have a few words with the postmistress and then get the hell home again.

Well, that *had* been Longarm's plan. Until he was shot at. Now he'd like some answers about other things, too. And this old boy with the ready rifle seemed just the fellow to supply that information.

Longarm shifted his Winchester into both hands ready to make a quick buttstroke to the back of the fellow's head.

He took a step forward.

And his left damned ankle gave out on him now that he didn't have the rifle to lean on for support.

Longarm fell sideways, hitting some trash on the ground and making one hell of a loud clatter.

The man with the rifle was still a half dozen paces distant when he whirled, frantically racking the lever down and then up again to load and cock his weapon while Longarm lay sprawled on his back on the ground like a bug flipped upside down.

"Shit!" Longarm bawled aloud as the rifle swung to bear in the direction of his belly.

Chapter 32

Son of a bitch's rifle barrel rapped the side of the door frame with a loud thump, the impact twisting the gun in the man's hands and bringing a curse to his lips.

Dammit to hell anyway!

Longarm couldn't take the time to hesitate. He dropped the unwieldy Winchester and snatched the Colt off his belt, it being much better in close quarters.

The Thunderer thundered and a great sheet of yellow flame lighted the alley for half a block in either direction. The 255-grain slug that rode the crest of that explosion slammed into the rifleman's chest and in the space of a heartbeat that individual lost all interest in shooting. His rifle clattered harmlessly to the ground, falling even while Longarm was busy triggering a second shot low in the man's torso.

The would-be assassin dropped to his knees and then toppled face forward into the dirt.

Longarm tried to scramble to his feet but the left leg simply would not support him. He gave up the attempt and rolled quickly to the side, but he needn't have bothered. The rifleman was paying no attention, and, in fact, was lying on top of his own weapon. He wouldn't have been able to grab it up and fire it if Longarm gave him until morning to do so.

Still, Longarm knew better than to make assumptions or to take chances. A hell of a lot of peace officers have been killed by "dead" suspects, just as an awful lot of careless hunters have been gored by the antlers of "dead" deer.

He could have made sure by putting a bullet into the man's head. But, dammit, he wanted this one to live. It's damn-all difficult to interrogate a corpse, after all.

Longarm crawled on hands and knees to the man's side and quickly frisked the wounded man, checking him for a belly gun or pocket pistol. He had a belly wound but no belly gun, and the only thing remotely lethal in his pockets was a cheap clasp knife. Longarm tossed that out of reach and rolled the man onto his back, then tugged on his rifle until it slid out from under his body.

The fellow was still alive and was sufficiently awake to know what Longarm was doing. He even did his best to raise his hips off the ground a little to make the task easier for Longarm.

"Am I dying?" he whispered.

"I don't know yet, mister. I'll need some light to see how bad you're hit." The words were intended to reassure or at least to avoid alarm. The truth was that Longarm did not need to see in order to know that the assassin had little time left to live. Longarm knew where his second, carefully aimed shot had gone. And that belly wound would be enough to kill, however slowly and painfully. He could also hear the hiss and soft, liquid bubbling of air moving in and out of a punctured lung in that chest wound.

If the man was lucky, he would drown in his own blood before having to endure the days of agony that a gut shot could bring. If he was lucky.

"Doctor," the fellow said, having to gulp for breath in order to form the word. "Need . . . doctor."

"There isn't any doc, I don't think, but there's a healer of sorts. I'll get her."

It was her house the shed was attached to. And come to think of it, she should've been out here by now. There'd damn sure been enough noise out here to raise her and any fresh dead laid out in the cemetery. If Harrisonville had itself a cemetery yet. And if there wasn't, well, this would be a fine time to start one.

Longarm was in no shape himself to go trotting around to the front of the house to fetch the healer. He settled for lying where he was and bellowing, "Help, dammit. We got a man wounded out here. He needs help. Bring a light an' come help, can't you?"

He shouted several times more before he saw the glow of lamps being lighted in the healer's house and in several others on the block.

A few more minutes and the alley was fairly well filled with curious women wearing coats over their night clothes, their heads covered by mob caps and several of them with knitted shawls even though the night was not cold.

Longarm didn't much give a shit how Druid women dressed for slumber, but he did care that when they came outside—hesitantly at first and then more boldly once they were sure the shooting was done with—most of them carried lamps or lanterns.

"Bring that light closer, will you? That's better." He sat up and shifted his butt closer to the wounded man. When Longarm pulled the fellow's shirt open he found pretty much what he expected. There was a dark red dime-sized depression in the man's pale flesh, but no bleeding to speak of. The blood would be seeping inside the body cavity where it would start the process of rot that seemed to occur when a man was shot through the intestines like this guy was.

The chest wound was similar except the blood there was a bright red made frothy by the passage of air in and out of the wound.

"Is it . . . bad?" the dying man asked.

"I've seen worse," Longarm told him. And hell, that was true. He'd seen men with their heads torn clean off their bodies. That was worse. So were a lot of other things he'd seen in his time.

None of the women was doing much to help, and so far there was no sign of their healer, so Longarm used the fellow's own handkerchief, which he'd found when he was going through the guy's pockets, to plug the hole in his chest. Immediately the man's shallow breathing eased and became almost normal.

The fellow smiled. "Thanks. That's better. I can tell."

Longarm nodded. He did not want to give false hope. But stuffing a bit of cotton inside a bullet hole was not going to do much except to stop the escape of air. He would still be bleeding inside and would die as soon as the blood filled his lungs. Longarm knew that. This man did not have to.

"I need to talk to you," Longarm said. "I got to ask why you came after me? Are you wanted for something? Did you think I came here to arrest you?"

The man gave him a wan smile and a slow shake of his head. Longarm was not sure what he was saying no to, but it was clear enough that he did not want to cooperate.

"Get me a lawyer," was all the fellow offered.

Longarm chewed on the problem for only a moment. Then he decided. "Mister, you aren't gonna be alive long enough to need a lawyer. You might as well tell me. Otherwise you'll die alone an' whoever put you up to this will walk away scot-free. Tell me, won't you?"

"You're lying," the man accused.

"Mister, I'm telling you straight. You're dying. Can you feel the heaviness in your chest? You ought to by now. You got ten, twenty minutes left, maybe. At least go out clean. Did somebody hire you? They must've. If you thought I was after you, you could've rode away after you shot at me an' missed. You came back, instead. Who are you working for?"

"I can't . . . tell you that. Gave my word, y'see."

"You're dying, mister. At least tell me why."

"Don't know . . . why . . . he wants you dead. Paid me . . . five hundred." A little blood appeared on the man's lips. "Do me . . . favor?"

"Why should I?"

The dying man ignored that retort and said, "Name is . . . Jorgensen. With an *e* and an *n* on the end. You know? Alex . . . ander Jorgensen. Got money in my wallet. Use that . . . to buy a . . . nice stone. Please?"

Longarm's impulse was to tell Alexander Jorgensen that he could go fuck himself. He did not. "Who hired you, Alex? Who's responsible for you dying now?"

Jorgensen only smiled. And turned his head away.

A few minutes later he was dead.

Longarm managed after several attempts to climb onto his feet. He used Jorgensen's rifle for his crutch.

He sent a venomous look to the women who'd stood silent and useless while Jorgensen died.

Longarm retrieved his own rifle and began limping back toward his camp beside the creek, fed up with the unhelpful miserable bitches who lived here.

Their so-called healer never had come outside, Longarm realized when he was partway back to the creek.

But then, she probably thought he was the one who'd been shot, he considered.

Damn them all, anyway.

Chapter 33

It occurred to him before he reached the edge of town that he was no longer nailed in place here among these mean-as-demons women. Alexander Jorgensen had had himself a horse. And since Jorgensen no longer needed that animal, Longarm now had a horse, too.

Longarm altered direction and headed back into Harrisonville, trying to remember the shortest route to the spot where Jorgensen tied the horse.

There was a damned strange thing happening on the main street of the town, he saw when he got back there.

Women were coming outside. Not just the ones that had come into the alley when Longarm called for help. All of them were coming out. He guessed that the ones who'd been in the alley went around knocking on doors or something once there was no longer a stranger in their midst. Or something.

However this came about, though, the whole town was awake now. They came outside in their night clothes, most of them carrying lanterns or, at the very least, candles. They flowed toward the center, toward the place where their Mother Corn lurked.

Longarm did not know if his presence would inhibit

them, but that seemed entirely possible. He shrank back into the deep shadows at the mouth of a narrow gap between two of the buildings and stood there watching while the women assembled all together in the night.

He guessed there were upwards of a hundred of them now that they were all out where they could be seen in a single bunch. A hundred, maybe fewer. But not fewer by much. He was sure of that.

They stood there for only a few minutes before four of the white-robed acolytes came outside carrying a very small litter—more of a sling than a litter, really—with Mother Corn in it. Either the old bag was too weak to walk or she had to be carried for ceremonial purposes.

And this was, he saw now, a ceremony of sorts that was developing here, never mind that it was the middle of the night.

Of course, for all he knew it could be that all their carryings-on took place at night. Which would make perfectly good sense. Any grown human with all his or her faculties damn sure ought to be ashamed to be exposed to daylight where they could be seen in such silliness.

Silliness it certainly was, Longarm figured, if they for some reason revered a cantankerous biddy like Mother Corn.

The Druid women arranged themselves in some sort of order, although by what means and for what reasons Longarm could not begin to divine. They certainly knew how to sort themselves out though, with Mother Corn and her bearers at the head of the pack, some other women— Longarm recognized the gray-haired healer called Lady Aster among them—close behind her, then another loosely organized bunch behind those and finally the lesser lights—common farmers, he supposed—bringing up the rear.

They all of them began to chant—wordless nonsense so far as Longarm could tell, although perhaps it meant

143

something to them—and to wend their way out onto the prairie grass apart from the town and the farm plots.

Longarm let them get well ahead and then trailed along behind. He didn't have to worry about losing track of them. With all those lamps and candles they were carrying, they looked like a swarm of slow moving fireflies against the dark, empty country that lay beyond the Harrisonville town limits.

Longarm couldn't make a lick of sense out of whatever this ceremony was. Maybe he could've if he'd been able to hear what Mother Corn was saying to them, but he was much too far away for that.

Slow and awkward as he was moving with his bum leg and only a dead man's rifle for a crutch, Longarm couldn't stay with the women. He had to settle for observing them from afar.

While he was at it, he went another block east and found Jorgensen's horse saddled and tied where the assassin left it. Longarm shoved his own Winchester into the saddle boot and tossed Jorgensen's rifle aside. That article was pretty much useless as a weapon now, since for the sake of comfort Longarm had been leaning on it muzzle down and using the wooden buttstock to hold on to. The barrel by now would be thoroughly plugged and incapable of firing until or unless it was given a damn good cleaning.

He kept the horse tied while he went around to the horse's right side and mounted. His left leg would not allow him to get on normally. The horse seemed unconcerned, but that was something a man doesn't know until he tries it. And Longarm didn't figure he was in any shape to be getting into a storm with a strange horse.

He set his feet in the stirrups and leaned down to untie the reins.

Lordy, but it felt good to be mounted and mobile again,

he realized. Better than he'd realized when he was stuck afoot here.

He eased the horse west to a spot beneath a roof overhang where the shadows were deep and he could look out to where the Druids were doing whatever the hell it was that they were doing.

Arranging themselves into this pattern or that and then slowly moving into a different pattern. That was all he could make out from a quarter mile or so distant.

They had stopped on top of a low mound. Not exactly an eminence, but the best they could manage close to Harrisonville if they wanted some elevation, he saw.

Mother Corn, still riding on the shoulders of her acolytes, was placed at the highest point. The rest of the crowd was milling around below her. Well, milling around was not a fair description. There was some sort of order to it all. He just didn't understand it. Wouldn't have from up close either, he supposed, although he would have liked to be able to hear what-all was being said out there.

He watched for a while, then concluded there was no point in him staying there.

He turned back toward the creek where he'd made his camp earlier.

He needed to retrieve his own saddle and things. Needed, too, to disable the snares and weir he'd placed. It wouldn't do to trap and kill and animal and then leave it there to die and rot.

Longarm figured he could attend to those small chores and still be at the HH Connected before Chubby called the hands to breakfast.

Chapter 34

Lordy, but it was nice to have real food again. The hands had already eaten and gone on to their can-see-to-can't-see workday while Longarm, at the foreman's invitation, hung around outside enjoying a cigar and a cup of stout coffee laced thick with canned milk and golden sugar.

"I know those women don't hold with meat in any form, Marshal," Billingsley had said, "so you wait until the boys are gone, then we can cook you up some proper grub. Fry some sausage to go along with the hotcakes, maybe."

"I don't want to put you out," Longarm protested.

"The boss said to treat you good, Marshal. He hasn't taken that back, not that I know about."

"You're mighty kind." He didn't push the refusal. Politeness required that he decline special treatment the first time it was offered. But it would've been stupidity for him to insist the second time. The mere thought of sausage fried in its own grease was enough to make his mouth water and his belly rumble.

Now Longarm sat at the table with Billingsley and Chubby, the three of them surrounded by plates of biscuits and platters of sausage that smelled like they fell out of heaven and tasted even better than they smelled.

"Fine sausage, Chubby. You make it?" Longarm asked around one huge mouthful while his fork was probing to stab the next bite.

The cook beamed with pride. "I do. It's antelope with plenty of beef tallow mixed in and sage and some other store-bought spices. Spent four years working up this recipe. Pack it in grease down in a thick crock so's it will keep and have it for our every Sunday breakfast. Haven't had a complaint about it yet. The boys go through it so heavy I have to put out a call for fresh antelope three, four times a year so's I can keep on making it."

"I don't doubt that for a minute," Longarm said. He finished off what was on his plate, then reached for more. And while he was at it, he helped himself to more biscuits, too, and some honey to drizzle over them. This was fine eating, he figured. All the more so considering the way he'd been treated by those damned women back in Harrisonville.

"How'd you say you got lost and come to ride back to us on one of our HH Connected horses?" Billingsley asked.

Longarm had just put a chunk of biscuit into his mouth. He almost choked on it when the foreman asked that of him.

Billingsley, for his part of it, looked like the question was of interest to him, but not terribly much so. He was paying more attention to loading the bowl of his pipe at the moment than he was to Longarm.

"I didn't . . . that's an HH horse? I didn't see a brand on it." Nor had he. That was one of the first things he looked for once there was daylight enough for him to see. The animal had a few scars on its chest and forelegs, but no brand that he could see.

Billingsley nodded and toyed with a sulphur-tipped lucifer. He couldn't light up inside the cookhouse, but it was obvious that he was wanting to smoke.

And Longarm now was wanting to talk. His belly was already close to groaning, so he pushed back from the table, leaving the rest of his biscuits and honey behind. He did, however, grab a couple crispy brown disks of that sausage to carry outside with him. He stood and plucked a cheroot from his pocket, motioning for Billingsley to join him. The foreman was quick to do so.

"Thanks, Chubby," Longarm told the lean cook on his way out. "I needed that." He grinned. "You may just have saved my life here." The cook looked pleased.

Longarm's easy manner remained once he left the building, but he was deadly serious about this conversation.

"You're sure that horse is one of yours?" he asked while Billingsley struck his match afire and held it over the bowl of his pipe.

"Sure, I'm sure," the foreman said, still not sounding as if the matter was of any particular importance. Longarm would have sworn the man knew nothing about someone riding on that animal to make two attempts on Custis Long's life. "Took a second look after you unsaddled and came over here this morning. It's one from a bunch of remounts we picked up last month. Fourteen head. Bought them off a fellow lives outside Buffalo. He raises some decent stock. Breeds enough for his own use and sells some surplus now and then. Haven't had a chance yet to brand these, but I was the one that took a crew down to Buffalo to collect them and drive them home here. We put them in a fenced trap over south there." He used the stem of his pipe to point toward where the unseen pasture would be found.

"Plenty of grass and water in there and the fence is good. Or was the last time I looked, and none of the boys has said anything about seeing wire down. If they had they'd've fixed it, of course, but I'm sure they would've told me about it, too, in case the staples were starting to rust out or we needed to keep a closer eye on it for some reason. I'm thinking now we must have a gap someplace or the horse wouldn't have got out. I'll have someone ride that line and see if he can spot what's happened, though."

Billingsley puffed on his pipe for a moment and asked, "Something happen to your horse, Marshal? Not that I mind, you understand. You're welcome to the use of anything on this place. But if you need your animal shod or something, just bring him in here. We'll take care of it for you."

"My horse is dead," Longarm said.

"Now that's a shame, but of course it happens. Can't keep an animal without it dying sooner or later unless you've sold it off first. Your horse looked young enough though. Break a leg or something?"

"Nope. Gunshot."

Billingsley's eyes involuntarily dropped to the Colt that rode on Longarm's lean belly.

"Nope," Longarm said again. "I wasn't the one that shot it. And it wasn't no accident, neither."

"Well, I know good and well it wasn't any of them women," Billingsley said. "I don't think any of them would know which end of a gun to hang on to or which to stand back of. When they first came by, we tried to loan them some rifles in case of . . . well, you know how it is. A man . . . or any other sort of person . . . is safer if he has the means to defend himself. And practically every ranch house between the Mississippi and the Pacific Ocean has a closet full of old .50-70 Springfields the Army wanted to get rid of. Government came along with wagon loads of the things, handing them out free just in case there was an Injun outbreak or something. We could've given the ladies a dozen rifles and never noticed they were gone. Those women all acted like we'd insulted them somehow. Like we'd stuck a chunk of raw, bloody meat under their noses and insisted they have a bite." He shook his head. "No sir, those women surely don't take to guns. Couldn't have been one of them shot your horse. I know that."

Billingsley frowned, then shook his head. "Can't think of anybody else that would've either. We've got some boys that are mischievous. You've seen that for your own self, Marshal. But there's not a mean-spirited hand on the place. Believe me, I make it a point to know things like that. My riders don't try and hurrah anybody nor shoot up the countryside for the fun of it. I won't have that sort of thing, and they know it. Anybody doesn't like the way I run this outfit is welcome to draw his pay and move on down the trail."

"Know a man named Alexander Jorgensen?" Longarm asked, his eyes fixed close on Billingsley to see how the foreman reacted to the name.

Billingsley's response to the name was as open and innocent as his prior conversation had been. He seemed to think about it for a moment, then shook his head. "No, I don't recall that I do."

"He doesn't ride for the HH Connected?"

Billingsley shook his head again.

"He was riding that horse of yours when he tried to kill me and shot my horse by mistake," Longarm said.

"Jesus!" Billingsley blurted.

"He was still on your horse when he tried for me again. Except this time I wasn't lying pinned underneath a dead horse."

"You don't have a prisoner with . . . oh." Billingsley looked genuinely shocked when he realized what that fact implied. There was no jail in Harrisonville any more than there were guns there.

"No, I don't," Longarm agreed without adding any unnecessary explanation. "Do you mind if I keep on using your horse for a spell?"

"No, keep it as long as you like, Marshal."

Longarm nodded and turned his attention to lighting his cheroot. His supply was running low by now, and pretty soon he would have to cut down on his smoking whether he wanted to or not.

But then he sure as hell hadn't expected to be out this long tending to the postmaster's 'simple' little job at Harrisonville, Wyoming Territory.

And—dammit—he *still* hadn't been able to speak with postmistress B. F. Lily.

Nor did he have the least damn idea why or who hired Alex Jorgensen to kill him.

The only good thing here was that Chubby's sausage was mighty fine.

Chapter 35

It seemed plain enough that he couldn't count on any sort of cooperation from those lunatic women in Harrisonville, and Roger Billingsley obviously was willing to help, but didn't know anything about it. Henry Harrison would be the next logical person to speak with, but he was off away from the ranch somewhere.

Longarm figured his next best bet would be to ride all the way back out to Cade's Station and see if Charlie Boyd knew anything about Jorgensen.

He saddled the as-yet-unbranded HH Connected horse and returned to the cookhouse to get Chubby to pack him a lunch. Heavy on the leftover sausage and biscuits, if you please. Which the cook did, happy that his efforts were being appreciated.

The rest of that day Longarm spent riding east, pushing the horse a little so he could reach Cade's Station at a reasonable hour.

He got there well past suppertime but not so late that he couldn't get a meal. By then he was hungry enough to eat Boyd's so-called squirrel stew, but it didn't come to that extreme. One of the Indian women remembered him from his earlier visit and fixed a thick steak for him without being reminded.

"Where's Charlie?" he asked.

The flat-faced, dark-skinned woman smiled brightly. And said not a word. No English, Longarm concluded.

Not that it really mattered. He knew Charlie wouldn't have gone far and neither was Longarm going anywhere, not until morning anyway. He surrounded the elk steak and motioned for a tot of whiskey to warm his belly while he waited for Charlie.

Boyd returned before midnight. It turned out he'd been no further away than one of his own back rooms. There were two very young Indian girls and a skinny Mexican senorita with him when he emerged.

Longarm smiled. It looked like at least some of Charlie's reputation was well earned.

"They should've told me you were here, Longarm," Boyd said. Then he laughed. "But I'll admit to being glad that they didn't. Have you been taken care of? Had something to eat? They gave you the good whiskey?"

"Yes," Longarm said, "to all of it, thank you. Tell me, Charlie. D'you have a few minutes to sit down an' talk? There's a couple things maybe you can help me with."

"Let me get a cup of sarsaparilla and a chunk of cheese, and I'll be happy to answer anything you care to ask. And if you like, I'll even make up answers for whatever I don't know." The way station proprietor ambled off toward the kitchen.

Longarm signaled for a refill and pulled out a cheroot. Cade's didn't carry the excellent cheroots he liked so very much, but he could resupply here with some reasonably decent brandy soaked crooks that would do until he found something better. After all, a smoke is much like a drink—or a woman—pretty much anything will do if there is nothing better available.

• • •

153

Charlie Boyd shook his head, his expression solemn for a change and serious. "No, I don't recollect any such name." He paused in thought again, but with no better result. "Jorgensen, you said."

"That's right. With an *e*."

"No. But then I don't always get a man's name. What does this Jorgensen look like?"

Longarm described the assassin. That brought a look of relief and a nod. "Now him I recall, all right. Except Jorgensen wasn't the name he gave me. Told me it was . . . let me think for a minute . . . Cratchet, I believe he said it was. Bob Cratchet."

"I don't s'pose this Cratchet mentioned having a son named Tiny Tim, did he?" Longarm asked sarcastically.

Boyd's response was deadpan and entirely sincere. "That has to be your friend, Long, for he did mention his boy. Little tike has something wrong with his legs and has to be on crutches, though I don't remember why nor what the boy's name might be. What about him?"

"He's dead," Longarm said.

"Aw, now that's a shame, leaving a crippled kid behind with no daddy to take care of him."

"Yes, isn't it," Longarm agreed, his voice dry.

"What is it you want to know about the gentleman? And say, which is his right name anyway? Jorgensen or Cratchet?"

"Jorgensen," Longarm said, positive about that, if nothing else. A dying man would want his own name on the stone, not that of some storybook character.

"Really? I wonder why he'd tell me that other. . . . Not that it matters. All I did was sell him a meal and give him directions."

"To Harrisonville?"

"No, to the HH Connected. He was asking how he could get to the HH Connected. Insisted he should go there even though I told him Mr. Harrison wasn't home at the time as he'd already passed through earlier in the day on his way down to Buffalo. Going to his lodge meeting, I believe he said."

"Uh huh. You were saying about Jorgensen? Or Cratchet, at the time?"

"That's about all I know to tell you, really. He came by, had some lunch and rode out again."

"Did you see his horse?"

"I did. He was riding a sorrel with three white feet and a blaze. Real tall and lean animal and not very broad in the chest."

"Did you see what brand it carried?"

Boyd shook his head. "If it had a brand I didn't notice. Wasn't no Injun pony though, I can tell you that. Had a roached mane and about the longest tail I ever saw on any horse. Had its tailbone broke and then reset, so it stood up tall at the butt and let all that hair flow behind when it moved. Moved real pretty, too. High stepping gait like it was snatching its feet up so they barely touched the ground before it popped them up high again."

"Did it always travel like that?"

"Hell, no. Tire a horse out in no time if you got it doing that way. No, that was a show-off gait. Cratchet liked to show the horse off though. He cued it into that gait when he knew I was looking. Once he rode off a way it settled down to a normal enough road walk. I know. I watched him go."

"On his way to the HH Connected," Longarm said.

"That's right. Though like I said, I told him Mr. Harrison wasn't home, and it was plain from looking at the man that he wasn't any cowhand looking for work. Soft hands. You know what I mean?"

Longarm nodded. "I know."

"Now you, you could handle cows. Probably have done sometime in the past, haven't you?"

"Uh huh."

"See what I mean? A body can generally tell. This Cratchet, or Jorgensen, he wasn't a cowman. But I'd say he knew his horses and had money to indulge his taste for good horseflesh. He was proud of that horse he had here." Boyd paused for a moment, then added, "But I'll tell you something else I thought about him at the time."

"What's that, Charlie?"

"I'd wager you a dried apple pie to a wet cow pie that he wasn't the one as trained that show-off horse of his. Somebody else trained it. All Cratchet did was pay so he could enjoy what someone else was capable of doing instead of him. But don't ask me how I come to believe that, Long, for I couldn't tell you why. I just believe it's so."

It was an interesting observation, Longarm thought. "Did it seem to you, Charlie, that Jorgensen was a city fella?"

"You know, now that you mention it, maybe that is what made me think that about the horse and everything. Yes, by George. I think maybe he is . . . was, I should say, may his soul rest in peace . . . a city fellow. I think you've put your finger on it."

Longarm grunted. Did not disbelieve Charlie Boyd, though. After all, Boyd had spent some time talking with Jorgensen. Longarm's only exchange with the man was by way of gunfire.

"Charlie, you're a big help, thanks." That was an exaggeration of considerable degree, but a harmless one. Longarm doubted that Boyd had contributed much at all to the solution Longarm needed here.

On the other hand, you tug on a single piece of thread and follow it to the end, you just may find yourself with the whole blanket by the time you're done.

And if Jorgensen had a high-stepping fancy horse when he left here, but was riding an unmarked range horse by the time he reached Harrisonville, could be there was a

156

n
w
lik
rem
  L
  Bu
drink

Chapter 36

Longarm woke early, well rested for a change and with his leg feeling considerably better as well. There was still a little tenderness in the ankle, but nothing he couldn't live with. The knee remained by far the worse of the two, but even it was much better than it had been. By wrapping some strips of cloth tight around the knee he could walk without a crutch or cane. Couldn't bend the knee real well like that but at least he wasn't so likely to fall down. Like he'd done the night he confronted Jorgensen.

He dressed and ate breakfast with a dozen or so coach passengers on their way north to Sheridan and Bozeman and eventually to Virginia City. The stage line seemed to do a good business along this route.

Breakfast was porridge and coffee. Longarm could have waited until the coach left and gotten Boyd's women to cook him up something better, but he did not want the trouble or the time that would require. He ate the porridge along with the others and helped himself to another cup of coffee when the jehu called them out to the coach. "All aboard or plan on staying a couple days." The passengers dropped their spoons and scrambled to regain their seats.

"You do a good business here, Charlie," Longarm commented once the coach had rattled and banged its way up the road.

"Yes I do, considering how far from everything this place is. Practically nobody around for miles. You going back west this morning?"

Longarm nodded.

"Can you do me a favor?"

"If I can, sure."

"The coach that just left here, it dropped off an envelope mailed to that Harrisonville place you mentioned before. It's over west, right?"

"That's right. Past the HH Connected."

"If it wouldn't be too much trouble, would you carry the envelope over there? God knows when there will be a regular carrier going that way, and I'm not paid to carry the mail. Hate to see it sitting around for months on end though."

"I'm not a postal employee, Charlie," Longarm protested.

"No, but you work for the government. That's practically the same thing."

Longarm probably ought to resent that assumption. But the truth was that carrying a piece of mail to someone in Harrisonville wasn't necessarily a bad idea. It would give him an undeniable reason to see postmistress Lily. And if anyone objected, not that he expected such, but if anyone did, well, he'd been assigned this job by the postmaster. That should count as pretty much the same thing as being deputized into post office service.

"Charlie, I'd be happy to carry that letter for you."

"Thanks. I appreciate it."

"How much do I owe you?"

"For supper last night and the room, then breakfast." He frowned in concentration. "Can't charge you anything for the horse seeing as it's mine. Dollar and a half should cover all of it."

159

"Put it on my bill, will you? But there's something I need to tell you about that horse I hired from you."

"What's that?"

Boyd did not seem excessively upset about the loss of his animal. And even less so when Longarm assured him the government would cover the loss for him.

"Fifteen for that, I think. I paid twelve. Got to make a little something on the deal."

"Fifteen is fair. I'll sign for everything when I come back through again."

Boyd nodded and fetched out a flour sack from beneath the bar. He handed the bag to Longarm.

"What's this, Charlie?"

"The envelope."

Longarm raised an eyebrow.

"I didn't want it getting spilled on or anything. You know."

Longarm did indeed know. In a country where mail was so very rare—and where so many folk could not read even if they were to receive a letter—it was often regarded as being downright precious.

Boyd performed his civic duty by making sure this envelope was in official hands, then went on about his business indoors while Longarm bought a few eatables to carry along with him this time and went out to saddle up.

Chapter 37

Longarm put up for the night at the HH Connected again. Decent bunk, decent hands, decent foreman, and damn good food. Not a bad combination.

"Say, you remember us talking about that horse of ours that your dead guy was riding?" Billingsley said before Longarm had a chance to take a conversation past the "Howdy" stage.

" 'Course I do."

"Well, I sent a couple of our boys over there yesterday to ride the fence line and see where that horse must've got out. Know what they found?"

Longarm grinned. "Let me take a wild guess. They found there's nothing wrong with your fence. And if they paid close attention I'd say they likely noticed a strange horse in with your band. Leggy sorrel with three sox an' some white on its face."

"Now how the hell did you know that?"

Longarm laughed. And told him.

"So that horse belonged to the fella you shot over to Harrisonville."

"That's right. Jorgensen, his name was. Do you still have the horse?"

"Sure. They brought it up to the corral for me to look at, in case I'd bought it without them knowing it belonged here. Got it over there still, if you want to look at it. No brand on it, though, if that's what you have in mind."

It was. But only partially. Longarm said, "Then I think I'll take it to use while I'm here an' let you have yours back. That way I don't have to worry about finding a way to return your animal to you when I'm done. And Jorgensen don't need it anymore. I'll figure out something to do with it once I'm done using it."

Billingsley nodded. "Is there anything I can do to help you?"

"If I think of anything, I'll damn sure let you know." Five minutes later, Longarm was asking for Billingsley's help. Alex Jorgensen's high-stepping fancy horse was scared shitless of somebody trying to mount from the right side. Wouldn't hold still for that even when it was tied tight to a hitching post. The animal fought so hard, Longarm was sure it was fixing to hurt itself. Or tear down half the HH Connected headquarters. Or both.

"Help me educate this son of a bitch," Longarm asked.

"You can keep on using ours if you'd rather."

"Not damn likely. The horse needs some manners."

Between a blindfold and Roger Billingsley twisting the sorrel's ear half off, they got the horse to hold still while Longarm climbed onto the saddle by way of the 'wrong' stirrup. And then up and down and up again half a dozen times more.

"All right, let's try 'er without the blindfold."

Billingsley took a fresh grip on the ear and pulled the blindfold off. The sorrel was still trembling and soaked with sweat in its fear, but Longarm managed to get on using the right side stirrup. He did it a good dozen times more, then had Billingsley hang on to the horse's head but let go of the ear.

"You think it will take to you mounting without help the next time?" the foreman asked.

Longarm grinned at him. "Damn if I know. But if you see a smoke signal in the west, you'll know it's me needing help again."

Billingsley laughed. Longarm gathered up his reins and put the sorrel into as smooth a road gait as he thought he'd ever sat, the horse stretching in a swift walk that was smooth as a porch swing and near about as fast as a man could sprint.

Except for needing just a little more work to make it useful out here in the real world, instead of on the bridle paths in some city park, this was one fine animal, indeed.

Longarm reached behind to make sure he still had the bag with the Harrisonville mail in it and gave the sorrel its head.

He ignored Mother Corn's unfriendly lair and rode straight to the post office. And if these crazy bitches wanted to keep horses off their precious main street, well, the hell with them. Longarm saw no reason to discomfort himself by finding a place out of sight where he could tie the horse.

There were no hitch rails along the street, so he made do by tying the sorrel to a pole supporting a porch roof in the same block as the post office.

Where, he was not very surprised to learn, there was no sign of the elusive Miss Lily.

He shook his head. What was it with these people? All he'd wanted was a couple words with one of them. Would they cooperate and do that? They would not. And now someone wanted him dead. Not that Longarm could see any connection between those two facts. But he surely did wish he could get shut of these women so he could concentrate on the much more pressing matter of attempted murder. That always interested him, and all the more so when it was his murder that was attempted.

Dammit, anyhow.

He walked into the post office and looked around again. As before, the place was empty. But, again, as before, someone had been here since his last visit. The printed forms and brown envelopes he'd seen the last time were gone now, and over at the far end of the work counter he saw one of those gray canvas ledger books that court clerks are so fond of.

This one—he limped over there and looked at it—this one seemed to be the Harrisonville voter rolls. That was reasonable enough, he supposed, since the paperwork he'd noticed before were all voter enrollment forms. Could be that Miss Lily was the town supervisor of elections as well as being postmistress. For damn sure, the woman didn't have to knock herself out with overwork in her post office capacity.

Longarm smiled just a little. A ledger of registered voters might very well include not only names but addresses. And if he could find postmistress Lily's address . . .

He dragged the heavy ledger to him and laid it open on the post office counter.

Humph! he sniffed. The whole damn first page was names beginning with the letter *A*. He needed the *L*'s. Which in a town no bigger than Harrisonville couldn't be but a page or two back, and . . .

Longarm frowned. Two pages in and he was still seeing names beginning with *A* and then a few *B*'s low on the right side. And none of these names were the same as flowers. So what the hell was this shit?

Oh, he could accept the idea that for something as serious as voting, the women might use their real names and not the made-up Druid crap. But . . . so many of them?

There were—he counted—twenty-four lines on each page. Forty-eight names on each left-right pair of pages then.

And there were—he thumbed through the book, counting as he went—there were nine pairs of pages completely

164

filled in and part of another page had been started. That was . . . he didn't try to work it out exactly, but rounding it off to fifty names per pair—that would be four hundred fifty names.

And the last names listed were only in the *N*'s. Hell, it looked like they had half the alphabet yet to go in their ledger. Call it eight, maybe nine hundred names if things held true to form.

A couple nights ago, Longarm stood there observing when the entire herd of Druids turned out for that candlelight ceremony out on the hill. He would have sworn there wasn't a soul left in town other than himself. Well, himself and Jorgensen, but he'd been dead and didn't really count.

There hadn't been a hundred head of them out there chanting and yammering and listening to their spiritual leader.

So where were all these people whose names were listed in the voter register?

Longarm could think of a simple answer to that question. But he sure didn't see *why* they would go and make up a bunch of phony registrations.

Which was what it sure looked like they were doing.

Mother Corn and her Druid women were faking voters. Making themselves out to be way the hell bigger a bunch than they really were. Why if they did a thing like that . . .

"Well, I'll be dipped in shit," Longarm exclaimed to the barren walls of the Harrisonville post office. "That sorry old bitch!"

He left the ledger lying open on the counter and went back outside to crawl very cautiously onto the horse—it shivered some but didn't go stark raving crazy this time like it had before when he tried to mount from the off side—and rode slowly out of town.

He wanted time and privacy where he could sit and do some serious thinking before he took this any further.

165

Chapter 38

Longarm ate the lunch Chubby had packed for him, then mounted and rode back into Harrisonville. The horse was on its best behavior, meaning it was still too scared to put up much of a fuss, so he was able to get on all right despite the weakness in his left knee. Keeping the knee tightly wrapped meant he couldn't bend the leg hardly at all and would never have been able to mount if he'd had to do it in a normal fashion.

He saw the pretty little farm woman chopping weeds near the edge of a tomato patch and waved to her, but got only a disapproving glare in return. He sure did wonder just who in hell it was who came into the shed with him a couple nights back.

Once again, he dismounted outside the post office and tied the horse there, then went inside.

"Well I'll be damned. Postmistress Lily, I presume?"

The woman was middle-aged, like so many of these Druids seemed to be, with gray-streaked hair done up in a pigtail tight enough to give her Chinese-looking slanty eyes. She wore a dress that was a good six inches too big around the waist for her and dragged the floor. Whoever that dress was made for, it wasn't her. She looked at him now, startled and blinking rapidly. "I am not."

"Of course you are," Longarm insisted.

"No, I am not. I . . . I never heard of anybody named Lily."

That whopper was outrageous enough to make him laugh. "Lady, you come around when I've got more time. I'll give you some lessons in lying. Believe me, you need the help."

"I am not the postmistress," she insisted.

"Who are you then?"

"I am the town supervisor of elections," she declared.

"What's your name?"

"Bonnie."

"Last name?"

"Francine."

"Initials B. F.," Longarm observed. "Like in B. F. Lily."

"I told you . . ."

"Yeah, I know. So you did. Doesn't make any difference right now anyway. I got mail here for the supervisor of elections." He opened the bag he'd carried inside and showed her the thick, weighty envelope that Charlie Boyd entrusted to him yesterday.

"Give it to me then."

"Nope. I'm not authorized t' do that, Miz Francine. I have t' give it to this Lily person. Then she can give it to you."

"But . . ."

"You swore to an officer o' the United States government that you ain't B. F. Lily. Care t' change your mind about that?"

The woman scowled at him. Then snapped, "All right, I am Bonnie Lily. Does that make you feel any better?"

He was tempted to rub it in a little by asking for some form of identification. But that would be ungentlemanly, wouldn't it? "Much better," he assured her.

"May I have the envelope, please?"

"Sure." He handed it over.

Postmistress Lily accepted it, then gasped when she looked closely at what she was holding. "It has been opened."

"That's right," he agreed, quite unnecessarily. He'd torn it open while he was having his lunch and the intrusion was blatantly obvious.

Longarm was not really up on the finer points of postal law. But if it ever came to that, maybe ignorance would work to his advantage this time. Besides, once he saw who the envelope was addressed to, he considered it to be potential evidence in a federal crime. Namely, an assault on a federal officer. And he being a federal officer in pursuit of a felon, identify as yet unknown, well a pretty decent case could be made to excuse his tampering with the envelope.

"It is only our packet of ballots. We have county elections coming up soon."

"Yeah, I saw that," he agreed.

"You are the one who opened the envelope then?"

"Ayuh. I'm also the one as thumbed through that ledger in the other room there," he said, pointing.

"You had no right. . . ."

"Lady, I have every right. I'm a federal officer here at the express invitation of the postmaster. But it ain't postal violations I'm thinking of right now. The crime I'm finding here right now has t' do with rigging an election. Which you stupid sheep are helping that old bat Corn accomplish. What d'you want to bet there's a bunch of you spends time in the territorial prison for it? Maybe worse time in the federal penitentiary if there's been any violation of postal laws, too.

"Now why don't you and me have us the talk I came here for. Then we'll both of us walk over an' have another chat, this time with Ma Corn. After that, I'll decide who I want to arrest an' for what."

168

Lily turned pale as a cotton boll and began to tremble. Somehow, Longarm thought he was going to have no trouble at all getting this sad, silly creature to tell him everything she knew.

Chapter 39

"But I really don't ... sir, I *swear* to you that I do not know *why* Mother Corn asks us to do this. Mother does not ... share with us ... the reasons she has for doing things, Marshal. She is a very spiritual person, you know. Her waters run very deep."

"Crooked, too," Longarm murmured.

"What was that?"

"Never mind." Longarm felt kind of sorry for Bonnie Francine Lily. The poor thing hadn't very much going on between her ears. Which was probably why she'd been chosen for this work. Suggestible, easily swayed with titles and flattery, getting poor Lily to do whatever Mother Corn wanted would have been about as difficult as convincing a kid to accept candy. "I think we can go have our talk with Cornhole now," he said.

"You should not be disrespectful of the Mother," Lily chided him. "If Mother Earth takes offense, you could be swallowed up and doomed to perdition."

"Sometimes I don't mind bein' swallowed."

"Pardon me?" Lily's eyes were wide and innocent. It was obvious that she genuinely had no inkling about what he'd just said.

"Never mind. It's not, uh, something you'd know about."

"Very well." She looked troubled. "Sir?"

"Hmm?"

"Could I . . . do I *have* to come with you to see Mother Corn? She may be angry with me. You don't know . . . she might raise her voice at me. I couldn't bear that. I really couldn't."

Longarm looked at the weepy, trembling thing before him and decided to give her a break. He already knew everything she could tell him. He supposed he didn't really have to have her in the room when he braced the old she-bitch in her lair. "All right. But stay right here. If I want you again, I don't want t' have to come looking for you or I'll do worse than raise my voice at you, I'll put you in handcuffs an' haul you down to the jail in Cheyenne."

Lily looked like she was fixing to wet herself. Longarm was not especially proud of being able to so thoroughly intimidate a middle-aged female half-wit. But it was something that needed to be done. He did not want the damned postmistress disappearing on him again. "Go inside the post office cage back there an' sit down. Stay right there until I come back for you."

"Yes sir, thank you sir," she put her eyes down and scurried into the back room.

Longarm shook his head. He was still confused about a lot of things. But now he understood why there was a post office in this weird community. The Druid members were not allowed to send or to receive mail. But they had to have a post office in order to send and receive voting information from the county seat over in Braddock.

So they built the building and secured Lily's official appointment. And since they had to have a carrier contract, they somehow got that through in Cheyenne, too. Except there was no Hysop Express Company. Not any more than there was a real and functioning post office. It was all part of the plan—somebody's plan—to influence elections in Crawford County and possibly in this whole north central chunk of Wyoming Territory. Longarm was far from being clear about all that.

But dear Mother Corn should have some answers. He figured to ask that sweet lady to share some of her knowledge with him.

Longarm stopped outside the post office to light a cheroot. Then, leaving the horse tied where it was, he strode along toward the old biddy's hole-up.

Chapter 40

"Young man, I am becoming quite weary of your boisterous entrances. Now will you please put those draperies
back the way you found them?" The woman who called
herself Mother Corn looked and sounded peeved.

But then, on her, a sour expression seemed perfectly
normal. Longarm found himself wondering if she ever
actually smiled.

Just for the record, so to speak, he fetched out his wallet
and opened it to display his badge. "I'm here on official
business."

"So you told me the other day," the old bag said with
a loud sniff. "Something to do with the post office. I must
tell you, I have no idea what has become of our dear little
Lily, and . . ."

"Stuff it!" Longarm snapped.

"I *beg* your pardon?" She looked like he'd slapped her.
Or worse.

"Beg all you please, it won't make no damn difference."

"Now see here, young man, I . . ."

"You'll shut the hell up is what you'll do. Either that

173

or I put you in manacles and haul you to Denver for questioning."

"You will do no such thing. You will . . ."

"I'll do what I got to do whether you like it or not. Now if you want to give me any more sass, speak right up." He brought out the set of steel handcuffs he carried in his back pocket and let them dangle where everybody in the room could see them. The sight had what one might reasonably call a riveting effect on all concerned.

In addition to Mother Corn, there were half a dozen of the acolytes in white robes, the healer Lady Aster and a couple women who he thought he'd seen before in the handicraft factory making dolls.

"I do not know . . ."

"You know as good as I do what's going on in this town," Longarm said in a tone of voice that was quite plainly accusatory. "More. An' now I expect you t' share that knowledge with me." He smiled, the expression not conveying so much as a hint of mirth. "The thing is, I know a good bit already. An' I don't figure to be telling you which bits I have an' which I maybe don't. So I'm gonna give you a general subject for you to talk on and let you say anything you like. But when I hear you tell me a lie, I'll put the 'cuffs on you. Tell me another after that one, an' there's no point in you telling me anything else, because I'll be carrying you down to Denver for arraignment and formal questioning whether you talk any more or not. D'you understand me?"

"Young man, I . . ."

Longarm raised his voice to a bellow loud enough to be understood above the roar of a cattle stampede on a stormy night—he'd had the experience and knew that to be a fact for certain sure—and roared, "Goddammit! Do. You. Understand. Me?"

Mother Corn physically recoiled away from him, shrinking back into a corner of her thronelike chair.

"The subject I expect t' hear about," Longarm said, "is voting an' elections hereabouts. Now you go ahead an' tell me all . . . an' I do mean all . . . about that, keepin' in mind what I said about you lying to me."

"Young man, I do not know what you could possibly be talking about. Voting, indeed. The Society has nothing to do with worldly matters like voting. We . . ."

She jumped a little when Longarm approached the platform where her throne commanded the place.

He could hear a chorus of gasps from the Druid women in the room when he reached out and slapped one of the cuffs around Mother Corn's bony wrist.

One of the acolytes fainted. Mother Corn herself looked like she probably would have fainted except she was so pissed off she probably didn't think of it.

"That will be quite enough, Deputy," a man's voice said from behind the throne.

A curtain parted and Henry Harrison stepped into view. Close on his heels was a thoroughly smug-looking Bonnie Francine. The little dummy hadn't waited where he told her, after all. She must have dashed for help as soon as Longarm was out the post office door.

But . . . Harrison? What the hell was he doing here?

"I'm pleased t' see you, Mr. Harrison," Longarm said. "Maybe you can help me talk some sense inta these people. I'm not for sure what-all they're up to, but I already know it involves vote fraud. They've falsified the town voter rolls with phony names, lots o' phony names, an' now they've got in the paperwork they need t' inflate the next election results till nobody will ever know what the decent people o' this county really want."

"Do you really think so, Deputy?"

"I know so. There's proof of it over in the post office. Let me finish putting manacles on the old woman then . . . which I shoulda done with Miss Lily there, I see now . . . an' I'll show you."

175

"That will not be necessary," Harrison said. "I believe you."

"Well, thank you, but I'd like . . ."

"Deputy," Harrison said, "you misunderstand me. I truly do not need to see your evidence. Because, you see, I am the party responsible for it being there."

"You are?"

"Indeed so. You are looking at the next senator to sit in the territorial legislature. And soon after that the next United States senator." Harrison smiled. "In a manner of speaking, Deputy, I am now your employer. It would behoove you to conduct yourself as you would your superior."

"That'll be the damn day, Harrison. I . . ."

Longarm heard the creak of a floorboard flexing somewhere behind him, and a moment later he felt a hard impact on the back of his skull.

He felt that. And then nothing at all.

Chapter 41

Longarm sat up. He was in the shed behind Lady Aster's house again. Enough daylight seeped through the gap around the door to tell him where he was. If this was supposed to be a homecoming of sorts, it was not one that pleased him. Of course, there was no jail in Harrisonville which would explain why, if he were to be confined, it would be here, where things were already secure.

And he was quite secure, dammit. He was bound hand and foot and his head hurt like hell, but he felt all right apart from those minor details. His Colt was missing, of course, and he had no idea where his Stetson had gotten to, but everything else about his person seemed intact.

There was a knife in his pocket, and if he could reach that. . . .

He could not. Whoever tied him did a lumpy, messy, ugly job of it. They used three, four times the amount of cord that was necessary. They also did it so damned thoroughly that he could not move his wrist far enough to the side to enable his hand to dip down into his pants pocket where the knife was. These women knew jack shit about tying or disarming a man, and, in their ignorance, they'd done a helluva fine job of immobilizing him.

Harrison must have stood back and let the Druids do it all.

But then Longarm supposed the politically ambitious rancher needed to maintain the fiction that Mother Corn was in charge here.

Damn him.

Corn knew perfectly good and well what was happening and seemed entirely content to let Harrison have whatever he wanted—votes—in exchange for what she wanted. Which appeared to be this autonomous, female-dominated enclave way the hell out in the middle of nowhere.

Just went to show what happened when women got the vote, Longarm grumbled to himself. The territory of Wyoming in its infinite lunacy had decided to grant that privilege to its women. Dammit. Longarm just hoped the federal government never became so deluded as to do the same on a nationwide basis.

As for Harrison's ultimate goals, God knew what those would be. He already had money. Now he wanted political power. If he ever got that, it would be Katy-bar-the-door. And all thanks to a butt-foolish Wyoming legislature and a batch of religious fanatics who worshipped the earth and the moon and shit like that.

Longarm was disgusted with them.

Mostly, though, he was disgusted with himself. He'd stood there like a little gentleman with a bunch of unreliable females at his back and got just what he deserved for being so stupidly trusting.

Now . . . well, now the price he would pay for that could be a little more than he really wanted to pony up.

No idea why he was still alive. But he would be willing to bet that Harrison and Corn intended to rectify that situation.

He wished he could reach his cigars and matches.

There were other things he wished also, but he didn't get those either.

Longarm rolled onto his back and drew his knees up to his chest. He was trussed like a hog ready for butchering, but he'd be damned if he'd lay there and let himself be taken that easy. If nothing else, he'd kick the sons of bitches soon as they came within reach.

The door swung open and the pretty little farm woman showed herself. She stepped inside and pulled the door shut behind her.

"Come to slap me again?" Longarm asked. "You needn't have gone t' all this bother, you know. I wouldn't've hit you back anyhow."

"Shush," she whispered. "I don't want anyone to hear."

"No?"

"No." She knelt beside him on the pallet and leaned over him, rolling him onto his side so she could get at his hands tied behind his back. He could not see what she was up to, but he could feel it well enough. She had a knife, and she was busily sawing at the cords on his wrists.

It took a while, there being so much material to cut through, but after a couple minutes his hands came loose. She crawled down toward his boots.

"Wait a second," he said. "You'll take forever with that dull knife. Let me do it." Now that he was able to get a hand into his pocket and get his own knife, his feet were free in another moment.

"Are you criticizing me?" she whispered.

"Lady, you're welcome t' do, say or act any way you like. If I didn't think you'd try an' knock my head off again, I'd kiss you."

"If we had time, I'd let you," she said. "Just not out in public where people might see."

179

"Listen, was it you that came t' visit me the first night I was in here?" he asked.

She gave him a deadpan look. But he thought he could see something of a mischievous twinkle in her eyes. "Sir, I have no idea what you are speaking about."

"Yeah, sure. It was you, wasn't it?"

She did not answer at all this time. But he thought it had been . . . or not. Maybe not. He just couldn't be sure.

Not that it mattered so very much. Particularly not at this moment. "Could you tell me what's goin' on out there?"

"The only thing I know, and that is only because I happened to overhear some of the acolytes talking among themselves, is that they are waiting for nightfall. There is supposed to be a sacrifice made by the Ladies of the Moon."

"An' that sacrifice would be . . . ?" He thought he already knew the answer to that one.

The little farmer shrugged. "You."

"Uh huh. Any idea where Harrison is?"

"Who?"

"Henry Harrison. He's the man that owns this land. Or did, till he gave it to your Society in exchange for certain small favors."

"Oh, there is no man here. We don't allow that."

"But you do allow blood sacrifices," he said.

The girl shuddered. "The thought of anything like that . . . it is vulgar. Profane."

"I have t' agree with that much," he said.

"We profess to revere life. How then can we take it? Not from a fish, not from a chicken, certainly not from a human being. That is why I came to free you. Now you can run away. Quickly, please. Before anyone discovers you are gone."

"Run away?" Longarm chuckled. "Lady, that'll be the day." He stood, stretching and flexing cramped muscles.

180

On an impulse he bent down and swept the farmer into his arms. She tasted clean, her breath sweet and her lips soft.

But he still wasn't sure if she'd been the one who sneaked in for that merry little romp the other night.

"Now, if you'll excuse me, I got a man t' see."

He stepped outside into the slanting light of late afternoon.

Chapter 42

Lordy, but he did wish he knew what they'd done with his Colt. He felt naked and more than a little vulnerable without it.

He had the Winchester on his saddle. But when he stepped around through the alley and peeped down the street toward the post office, all he saw was street. And buildings. He'd left the sorrel tied outside the post office. It was not there now. Dammit.

He hesitated only for a moment. The choices seemed clear enough. He could stumble around Harrisonville looking for the horse, leaving himself wide open to discovery by any pair of eyes in town. That would give Harrison and Corn enough warning to bushwhack him from a distance. Or he could take the play to them with him dictating time and place. More importantly with him deciding what kind of separation there would be between himself and Henry Harrison. Harrison had Longarm's Colt and Winchester in addition to whatever weapons he normally carried. If any. That didn't matter, though, since Longarm knew he had Longarm's own guns at the very least.

The point was, the closer Longarm could be to Harrison

when the showdown came, the better it would be.

And so, he decided, better now for him to be the hunter and those SOBs, male and female alike, the prey.

He did slip back deeper into the alley long enough to pull out a cheroot. The slim, near black little cigar was the last of his good stock. After this, he would have to smoke the brandy crooks he'd gotten at Cade's Station . . . if he was still alive to worry about such things, that is. He took his time about trimming, moistening and warming it before finally striking a lucifer and building a coal. Damn, but that smoke did taste fine. He drew it deep, held it a moment and then slowly let the smoke trickle past his lips. Nice. Very nice.

He jammed the cheroot into his mouth, took a deep breath . . . and a'hunting he did go.

"You! You can't . . . You aren't . . ."

Longarm didn't much give a shit what the woman thought he couldn't or wasn't. He strode boldly forward and grabbed hold of the heavy draperies that protected the sanctum sanctorum of the Druids from the intrusion of sunlight.

Before, he'd swept those curtains wide to make his entrance.

This time he parted them, took one in each hand and ripped the sons of bitches clean off the rod that held them up.

The curtains tumbled to the floor in an untidy heap, and Druids began to squeal with alarm. They sounded like a bunch of squeaking rats, he thought.

In the harsh light of day, Mother Corn's lair looked shabby. The black paint on the floor was scuffed and starting to flake, and the place needed sweeping out.

The acolytes looked like they were going to faint. Then one of them did faint, and the others went scurrying away, leaving that one flopped on the floor.

Mother Corn looked scrawnier and meaner than ever. She had to be a hundred fifty years old if she was a day. Had enough wrinkles to make him believe that anyway.

And it was no damn wonder she wanted the place kept dark all the time. The old bitch was wearing a wig—a badly made wig at that—that had thin, pale wisps of her natural hair escaping around the edges. It looked like she had almighty little in the way of real hair left. Mother Corn, the old hag, was going bald.

"What'd you do with my handcuffs?" Longarm demanded as he crossed the room and stood immediately before her. "You're under arrest. I'm taking you in." He didn't try to enumerate the charges. He would think of some later. He was sure there would be a good many he could choose from, all the more so once he got the Justice Department's lawyers and the Wyoming territorial officials in on the act.

He had to give the wrinkled old piece of shit credit. She didn't scream nor cry nor bluster. She lifted her chin and glared at him, drawing herself up to as much height as she could manage on her chair.

"Henry!" she bellowed in a voice ten times louder than Longarm would have thought her capable of making.

Perfect, Longarm thought. Just perfect.

A moment later Henry Harrison stepped out from behind the curtain across the back of the room.

He had Longarm's Colt in his hand, and the gun was pointed squarely at Longarm's belly.

"This is as far as it goes," Harrison declared.

"Yes, by God, so it is," Longarm responded.

Harrison's thumb went to the hammer of the big Colt. It was a double-action revolver and did not have to be cocked manually, but apparently Harrison did not know that.

Not that Longarm cared either way. He did not consider himself the one in danger here.

Longarm dipped into his vest pocket and came out with the two-shot .41 derringer that he carried on the fob end of his watch chain.

The little gun's bark was loud, and it twisted in Longarm's hand.

The bullet struck Harrison in the chest. He gasped and went pale, his expression slack and his knees wobbling. The man staggered but managed to keep his feet.

"Drop the gun, Harrison. You're under arrest. Now drop the gun an' I'll take you in. Get a doctor for you, too."

Harrison looked at him. The man gasped, "You've ruined everything. Everything."

He raised the Colt and tried to take aim with it.

Fuck him. Longarm cocked the derringer again and aimed with care, then sent his second bullet onto the flat plane of Henry Harrison's forehead, immediately above the bridge of the ambitious gentleman's patrician nose.

Harrison's head looked like it was trying to expand, and blood began to flow out of his ears and nose and eye sockets. There was no dramatic spray of brains, though. But then the .41 rimfire cartridge didn't have near the punch of a reliable old .44-40 or .45 Colt.

The comparison was entirely academic, of course. By the time Longarm noticed those things Henry Harrison was lying facedown on the floor, dead as a shoat in the oven.

Longarm stepped forward to recover his Colt from the dead man's hand.

Before he reached the body, however, he was halted by the ominous *ca'clack* of a gun being cocked.

Mother Corn, incredibly, held a carbine in her hands. It must have been lying on the dais beside her chair. She was aiming it at Longarm. She didn't look particularly adept with the rifle. But then there was only a half dozen feet between them. Marksmanship was not required.

"Don't!" Longarm snapped at her. "Don't."

The old bitch was going to. He could see it in the tension at the corners of her eyes and in the way her mouth pursed with anger and determination.

"Don't," he warned again.

The Druid hag paid him no mind. She gritted her teeth, whatever of them remained, and yanked the trigger.

The rifle exploded with a metallic, ringing bang.

Not fired, that is. Exploded. The real thing. As in . . . the Winchester blew up.

Splinters of brass and steel erupted from the breech end of the rifle and flew like shrapnel from an artillery shell.

Corn's right hand was blown completely off and her left forearm was shattered. A twisted bit of steel sliced her cheek open, dropping the flesh away like an apron to expose her teeth in a ghastly caricature of a skull. Another entered one eye and lodged somewhere back in the recesses of her brain.

Longarm shook his head and took a moment to examine himself. He was unharmed even though he'd been standing six feet in front of the muzzle of the rifle.

But the rifle, as he'd tried to warn her, was the one that had belonged to Alexander Jorgensen.

And when Longarm used it as a cane he'd used it muzzle down. The front end of the bore had been full of mud and gravel, packed in and dried over a period of several days.

The powder charge in the cartridge was unable to clear the obstruction, so the cartridge case ruptured and the entire explosive content of the cartridge was released into the rather weak breach mechanism.

The result was messy but damn-all effective.

Longarm took one more look at the dead woman, then bent to retrieve his Colt.

There was no sign of the Druid women who'd been in the room a few minutes earlier.

186

Probably they'd gone somewhere to pack their things. They might as well do so, he thought, for he strongly suspected the town of Harrisonville, Wyoming Territory, was about to disappear. And before it ever made it onto the maps, too.

No loss there.

He figured he would have to find his horse and gear, then probably clean out the stamps and shit in the post office so they could be returned to whoever was supposed to take charge of such things.

He did have one regret, though.

He surely did wish he could find out for sure if that pretty little farm girl was the one who'd come to him the other night.

Watch for

LONGARM AND THE BLACKMAILERS

287th novel in the exciting LONGARM series
from Jove

Coming in October!